THE LAST SÉANCE

Dark Covenant Series Book 1

DEAN RASMUSSEN

The Last Séance: Dark Covenant Series Book 1

Dean Rasmussen

For more information about this book, visit:

www.deanrasmussen.com
dean@deanrasmussen.com

The Last Séance: Dark Covenant Series Book 1

Published by: Dark Venture Press

Cover Art: GetCovers

❀ Formatted with Vellum

❧   1   ❧

The bell above the door rang and Nora flinched. They weren't expecting any clients that early. She cut her conversation with her sister, Ally, short and turned to face a black-haired thirty-something man who'd stepped into the parlor. He met their gaze for a long moment as if deciding whether or not to stay then pushed the door closed behind him.

"Madame Lenora?" he asked.

"Yes." Nora stepped out from behind the front counter. "I'm Madame Lenora."

"I need a séance… for my daughter."

The man's hair was a mess, his eyes were bloodshot, and his gaze focused on something beyond her. She'd seen that same look in some of her clients, most often the result of debilitating grief, but there was something else in his eyes. Severe trauma? PTSD? Drugs? The smell of smoke hung in the air as he approached. It wasn't cigarettes, but something else she couldn't quite place. Sweat glistened on his pale face.

"My sister and I would be happy to help you contact a loved one," Nora said. "Sorry to hear of your loss."

His mouth and eyes squeezed shut for a moment before he

answered, "I need to speak with her today, right now. No bullshit."

"I'm sure we can make that happen."

Slipping off his gloves, he stuffed them into his coat pockets. "I need to tell her something."

"Of course," Nora said, stepping forward.

His eyes watered. He held out a wad of cash, practically stuffing it into her hands, yet she hesitated to accept it. Glancing back at Ally, she watched as her sister switched seamlessly into sales mode, pointing to the sign on the counter.

"Our services are listed here," Ally said in a sweet, gentle tone. "A thirty-minute séance is a hundred dollars, and we offer a lot of other services: guided meditation, palm reading, fortune telling—"

"Nothing else," he said. "Can we please start now?"

"Yes, of course." His appearance and urgency unsettled her.

"She died recently?" Nora asked, if only to stall for a moment.

"Does it matter?" he asked.

"No, not really."

He gestured to the cash. "It's all there."

"That's fine." Nora glanced over at Ally, who was watching everything curiously. Her sister's eyes narrowed—she was sizing him up.

"You have to help me," he said. "The sign outside promised..." He read the words verbatim. "*Genuine psychics with a heart. Gateway to the afterlife.*"

"I'm happy to help you," she said, finally accepting the cash with a smile and extending her hand. "I'm sorry, but I didn't get your name."

"Gabriel Flores." He stared intently with bright green eyes while shaking her hand. His grip was firm—a little too strong— and she pulled away quickly. His hands were freezing, and the smell of sweat drifted off his clothes.

He leaned forward and stared into her eyes for a long

moment. "I want to see my daughter again. Can you make that happen?"

"I can't promise you'll *see* her," Nora said. "Physical manifestations are rare, but a conversation usually happens, unless—"

"Unless what?" The man furrowed his brow, and his face tightened in frustration.

"Unless... the spirit refuses."

"Why would she refuse?" Gabriel asked. "She's my daughter."

"Not to worry," Nora said. "I'm sure we can communicate with her."

"How?"

She offered a reassuring smile. "She will speak through me."

"I want to hear her voice."

Nora nodded. "I'm sure it won't be a problem, except it won't sound *exactly* like your daughter's voice. Her words will come through, but—"

"Then how will I know it's real?" He grimaced.

"Family members usually come through quite well. I've got a lifetime of experience. The Vale family is known for its psychic abilities. Is that why you chose us?"

He let out an exasperated sigh. "Can we start this now? I want to talk to her." The frown on his face deepened.

Nora turned to Ally. "Prepare the room, little sis."

Ally nodded, brushing a strand of long brown hair behind her ear, and hurried away toward the back of the parlor. Instead of heading into the séance room, she disappeared through the door just beyond it—the control room.

Nora pointed to the coat rack in the corner. "There's a place for your jacket."

He shook his head and folded his arms across his chest. "I'll keep it on. I'm so cold."

She glanced down at his heavy-duty boots. They were scuffed and salt-stained but perfectly suited for the harsh Minnesota winters. Despite his outward appearance, he was difficult to read. Walk-ins were tricky. Extracting clues about someone's personal life that she could use to her advantage during the séance was critical, and sometimes it took a carefully worded conversation to paint a clear picture of their background and situation. Often, she had time to do a little research on her clients, with Ally's help, but walk-ins presented a challenge every time.

Nora turned back toward the front window that faced the street. The frost had spread beyond the corners from the previous night as the temperatures had dropped into the single digits. "It *is* horrible outside, I know," she said. "The worst part of living in Minnesota, but I'm sure you're used to it by now... if you grew up here."

"Please," he said. "I'm so tired. I need to speak with my daughter."

"Of course." Nora swallowed. "Follow me."

She would need to improvise more than usual.

Leading him down the hallway, they turned into the séance room. She directed him where to sit at the table, and he dropped into his chair, scrutinizing her every movement.

She dimmed the light as she'd done a hundred times before but kept it a little brighter than usual. The client's incessant stare unnerved her.

As she gathered a bundle of sage, she lit the leaves with a wooden match and watched them blacken and curl until they caught fire. Bits of its sweet scent drifted into the air. She blew out the sage and let the embers glow, the tendrils of smoke unfurling into the air.

This is what every client demanded of her—the attention to detail, to show she was an authentic medium who suffered for her craft. Someone who could reach into the darkest corners of the afterlife and wrestle with dark forces to contact their deceased loved ones.

They all wanted something real, something dramatic, something emotional. So she never held back.

Waving the bundle of sage slowly around the table, she

settled into her antique velvet chair and faced her client. Judging by his wide eyes, he was a believer. His nervous gaze followed her every movement. A fire of desperation radiated from his face, something she'd seen so many times before. She knew that look: the pain and longing of a tormented soul.

She drew circles in the air, then swept over the obsidian mirror that sat on the table between them. She moved it around herself, breathing in the smoke deeply to show him that she was fully invested in making his request a reality. It was all part of the show.

After placing the bundle in a small brass dish beside the three black candles on the table, she lit them and positioned them in a triangle around the obsidian mirror. With a bit of dramatic flair, she ran her fingers along the edge while letting the flames dance for a moment. Glancing up, she met his gaze while extending her hand.

"Do you have something that belonged to your daughter? Maybe a piece of jewelry, a doll, or even a picture?"

He glanced down, then reached into his pocket and pulled out a small plastic sandwich bag. Several strands of long black hair sat clumped in a corner. He handed it to her with a bit of reverence. "A lock of Anna's hair."

"Perfect." She took it, opened the bag, and pinched a small section of it between her fingers, bringing it out and placing it in the center of the obsidian mirror. "Anna. What a beautiful name!"

It wasn't ideal that she didn't have much information about her client. It was possible he still might disclose a little more about his daughter before she started—*anything* to set her on the right path—but instead he silently stared back at her. She would need to improvise a little more than usual.

"Are you ready, Mr. Flores?" she asked.

He nodded. "Yes."

"You must remain still throughout the process," she said.

"Of course. I won't move."

"Whatever you do, don't interrupt me—that will break the connection—and don't speak their name unless I request it."

"I won't," he said.

Nora nodded once. "Then we'll begin."

She stared into the obsidian mirror and took a deep breath. Tracing the mirror's rim with the tips of her fingers, she spoke in a deep whisper, "Anna."

At the sound of his daughter's name, Gabriel flinched. He leaned forward and stared down into the mirror with wide eyes as if he might also get a glimpse of what she was seeing. The silence stretched on between them for a few seconds to build more tension before she narrowed her eyes so they were almost closed.

"Anna is near," she said. "I'm afraid she's surrounded by darkness."

Gabriel let out a muffled moan but didn't say a word.

"Anna," Nora said. "Your father is here. He wants to talk to you." The table rumbled to life, and the candle flames wavered a bit. She continued in a hushed tone, "I can feel her presence."

"Is she here?" He broke in, glancing around the room. "I'm sorry, but I need to know."

"She's here, but you won't sense her like I do. She says she misses you."

He gasped and tightened his grip on the edge of the table. His eyes watered. "I miss her too."

Nora stared into the obsidian mirror, while dwelling on any comparisons between Gabriel's daughter, Anna, and Nora's own daughter, Lucy. She guessed both girls were around the same age, with the same interests, and judging by Gabriel's impassioned pleas to talk with Anna, she had played a pivotal role in his life. They must have been very close, as Nora was to Lucy. Maybe this wouldn't be so difficult after all. Just bring up the special moments she'd shared with Lucy.

"She says she remembers how you used to sing her lullabies at bedtime," Nora said.

Gabriel gasped, louder this time. "Yes," he whispered, "I did, every night."

"She says to keep her drawings. Don't throw them out."

"I'll never throw them out."

"Do you know... she's right here, standing beside you." Nora glanced into his eyes to gauge his reaction. He was trembling a bit, his hands folded over on top of themselves on the table. His fingers were scratched and dirty, and he was rubbing them together nervously. Things were progressing nicely. Then she leaned forward and took it up a notch. "She wants you to know she still hears you."

A tear streaked down Gabriel's cheek. It always happened this way. As soon as she mentioned a loved one in their presence, they would start crying. It was only human—a sort of therapy for her clients. A time to heal some of the grief they'd built up since their loved one had passed away.

Normally, she gave them time to let it all out, to recover from the overwhelming emotional release of the moment, and, normally, she looked away to give them a bit of privacy. But this time, she couldn't. There was an emptiness in his eyes. Anna's death had eaten away at his soul. He'd been suffering for a long time.

Gabriel's eyes sparkled in the flickering light from the candles. His drooping face had lit up after sharing her words with him. A pang of guilt swept through Nora. She had given him false hope, like all the others, but he was taking it to heart in a deeply personal way. She had ventured into uncharted territory. Still, this is what he had paid for, and she had delivered.

Pushing away the guilt, she stared down into the mirror and focused on her performance again. "What would you like to say to your daughter?"

He struggled to speak between tears and stared longingly into the mirror. "I miss you so much, Anna."

A soft voice came from every direction—through the carefully placed speakers around the room—Ally's digitally altered voice. The haunting voice of a young girl. Her words echoed and wavered in the darkness. "Daddy, I miss you so much too."

"Anna," Gabriel cried out. "Is it really you?"

"Yes, Daddy. It's me."

Gabriel tried to speak again, but the tears cut his words short. Gasping and clearing his eyes, he spoke in a raspy voice. "It's... It's hard to go on without you."

"I know, Daddy," came the girl's voice. "But I'm fine. I'm happy here. We'll be together again someday."

"We will." Gabriel nodded. "I promise."

Nora looked up and was startled to see that he was staring at her. The tears had left long trails down his cheeks, and he wiped them away with the back of his hand. "I want to see her."

The request caught Nora off guard. This wasn't possible. Her visual illusions were limited to the usual practical effects found in most psychic parlors around town.

She tried to let him down easy. "I'm sorry. The spirit isn't making it possible for me to manifest her. Do you have any other questions?"

"I do." He stared longingly into the mirror, watching the candlelight dance over its surface. "Please forgive me, sweetheart. I tried everything to save you. I really did. I'm so sorry."

Anna's voice seemed to sweep around the room. "I forgive you, Daddy."

"Ask her if she can please hold me now," Gabriel said. "One last time. Tell her to put her arms around me and hold me as long as she can. I need to feel her presence again."

Nora's heart ached from his impassioned plea, but there was no way she could make his request happen. "I can try," she said anyway, glancing to the side over her shoulder.

Ally would be watching them from her position just out of sight behind the small one-way mirror. Maybe she could do something extra to enhance the experience for this client—say something sweet again in Anna's voice, release a burst of warm air, or adjust the lighting a bit to give him a greater sense of connection with Anna, even for a moment. She *really* hoped Ally was watching and would improvise.

Leaning forward, she took his hands and formed a circle around the mirror with their arms. "I'll do my best."

He squeezed her fingers a little too tight, but she held on and tilted her head up.

"Anna," she said, "please grant your father's request and let him feel your presence, if you can."

A slender thread, almost imperceptible within the dim light, dropped behind Gabriel and moved closer toward the back of his neck. It extended to the ceiling. Ally had come through, providing a simple yet effective technique they'd used on previous occasions. The thread's delicate touch would be enough to satisfy him.

"Close your eyes," Nora commanded.

He nodded, pulling his hands away briefly to wipe his tears. He sniffed but remained silent and then clutched her hands again. When the string touched his back, his spine straightened and his mouth dropped open, although his eyes remained closed as the string swept across his back. He gasped. "Anna!"

The thread brushed against him again, and Gabriel spun around. He lifted his hands into the air as if to catch Anna's spirit but snagged the thread instead. The thread, the wooden mechanism holding it, and a section of the false wall separating them from Ally came down with it. Everything crashed to the floor with a thud.

Gabriel twisted in his chair to look around, but Nora pulled him toward her.

"What was that?" Gabriel asked in a weak voice.

"Spirits can be unpredictable," Nora said quickly. She stared at his closed eyes, hoping to keep his attention long enough for Ally to sneak in behind him and sweep away the thread. Her heart pounded a little faster as she spoke in a louder voice to cover for Ally. "Sometimes their energy—"

He turned around suddenly and stared at the floor. The

thread had pooled on the back of his shoulder, and he reeled it in slowly, at first, his face full of confusion. "What's going on here?"

"Mr. Flores, please—"

He turned back to her and stared with an intensity she'd never seen in anyone before. His eyes were still wet and blood-shot from all the tears, and he shook his head. "Did you do this?"

She shook her head. "Something must have fallen from the ceiling. It's not part of the—"

"What is this?" he asked again.

"Please, Mr. Flores, let's concentrate on your daughter. She's still here despite the distraction."

He shook his head again as his expression drooped. "This is a lie, isn't it? None of this is real."

"We'll start over."

"Not again," he said. "Not again, not again." He pulled away from the table and stared up at the ceiling where one of the panels had broken loose. "Is somebody up there?"

Ally was silent, of course, and judging by the stillness, she had frozen in place.

Gabriel's voice grew louder and shriller. "You're scamming me, aren't you?"

"Nobody is scamming you, Mr. Flores."

"You're lying." He tugged at the ball of thread in his hands. "Tell me the truth. Was that my daughter's voice just now?"

"It was her," Nora said. "I have to end the session now."

"Because it was *never* her, was it?" His eyes started watering again, dropping the ball of string. "Please tell me that was truly her."

"It was, I swear."

"Liar!" He stood suddenly, knocking his chair over and leaned toward her with bared teeth. "Anna is gone forever, isn't she? Nobody can bring her back to me."

"We can try again."

He seemed not to hear Nora now and continued, "She's gone. My Anna is gone. I've lost everything."

"I—" Nora held up her hand, trying to calm him.

He lunged forward without warning, his fingers locking around her arm with a brutal force that sent a jolt of pain through her neck and head.

He'll break it in half.

She tried to rip away from him, even as he reeled her closer. The twisted look on his face sent a chill through her body. His wide eyes had grown to circles, and the smell... the sweaty smell of his body filled her nostrils. Throwing her weight back into her chair, her shoes scraped across the tiled floors. He grabbed her sleeves. Pounding at his hands, her dress ripped, and she let out a deafening scream.

"Nora!" Ally yelled from somewhere behind the walls.

The look in Gabriel's eyes... lost, empty, dead.

He let her go, then staggered toward the front room, screaming obscenities all the way. "Go to hell, all of you! Fucking liars! Goddamn you all to hell!"

Instead of calling the police, Nora hurried after him. "Please, Mr. Flores."

He turned back with a gaze that seemed to bore a hole through her. "My dead daughter is a parlor trick to you?"

Nora swallowed and tried to soften the tone of her voice. "It's not like that at all."

"Bullshit." He shook his head. "I lost everything. How could I have been so stupid to believe in any of this?"

A booming voice cut through the tension from behind them. "No refunds!"

Nora turned as her father came charging out of the back room, stomping forward with his cane and broken posture. "Get the hell out of my shop before I call the police."

"Fuck your money," Gabriel said. "Rot in hell, goddamn scam artists."

"Nobody talks to us like that!" Her father's hand slipped to his side as if suggesting he was armed. "We run a professional business here."

Gabriel backed away, and his expression changed. It wasn't rage this time, but something deeper, like his heart had exploded. "You don't understand what it's like to lose everything."

Nora's father inched toward the man, putting himself between them. "We deal with loss every day, and you have no right to accuse my—"

Before her father could finish, Gabriel stormed out the front door, slamming it so hard that the front picture window rattled in its frame. Nora cringed, waiting for it to shatter.

As soon as Gabriel was gone, the room seemed to grow colder. Not just that the front door had let in a burst of winter air, but something that chilled Nora to the bone. Had someone switched off the heating system?

Only a moment later, Ally rushed into the room. "I'm so sorry," she said. "I... I dropped it."

Nora's father burst out, "Dropped it? There's no room for mistakes in our business. If it happens again—"

"Dad," Nora cut in, raising her voice. "It won't happen again."

Her father grumbled, looked at both of them, then trudged back into his apartment.

She waited until the sound of his cane thumping against the floor was gone before she turned back to Ally. "It's not your fault."

"I'm sorry," Ally said. "I haven't used that contraption for a long time. It's an old trick."

"We'll figure out something else."

Ally touched the torn sleeve of Nora's shirt. "Are you hurt?"

She shook her head. "Only my pride."

❧   2   ☙

Nora stared into the obsidian mirror at the center of the séance table. The flickering flames from the candles on the shelf behind her reflected off the mirror's polished surface. The scrying mirror, the Ouija board, the tarot cards—all of it was just a bunch of props, like her. She'd even dyed her hair black to give her persona, Madame Lenora, a little more mystery. It was just another day to dazzle the believers, to throw herself into a role she had long since lost faith in. Everyone came searching for answers, but she had nothing to give them. Nothing *real* anyway. Still, they hung on her every word, their desperate gazes absorbing her performance as if they'd caught a glimpse of the afterlife.

"I bring less light into this world than this candle," she said.

"Sulking again?" her father's booming voice came from the doorway.

She shuddered but didn't glance over at him. "Don't sneak up on me."

"What are you afraid of? Ghosts?" He gave a little laugh.

"Go back to your apartment. The clients will be here soon."

"Not according to Ally. Only thirteen bookings last week. That's less than three per day. What's going on?"

She made a wide gesture around the room. "You think my customers enjoy coming back here? It's a time capsule straight out of 1978. It's a shithole."

"A good performer learns to use the tools at hand," her father said from the doorway. "Your mom and I never needed fancy computers and electronics to put on a good show."

She met his gaze and looked into his eyes for a long moment. A cigarette dangled from his fingers, although it wasn't lit yet, thank God.

He had stopped by again on his way out the parlor's back door, where he usually stood in the alley to smoke and complain to anyone who happened to step too close to him. It was difficult enough to keep the air filled with sweet incense, to give it that authentic flavor her clients loved so much.

The cigarettes had taken their toll on him over the years. He'd lost most of his self-described *charisma*—code for asshole— after a mild stroke had knocked the wind out of him. His cane reminded her of the punishments she'd endured beneath his belt, punishments she rarely deserved.

He was hunched forward now, frail and thin, his gaunt face staring back at her, full of deep lines. He still held a powerful presence, with a calculated stare full of judgment and wrath if she made the wrong move.

"The clients demand more these days," she said. "They love the new stuff Ally bought, especially the electronics she's working behind the scenes."

"It's not all the fancy gadgets," he said. "It's the conviction in your eyes. The way you move through a room. That's what they like. They're paying for the drama."

She turned away and rolled her eyes. "I know what I'm doing. You can go back to your apartment now."

He was silent, but he didn't leave.

She avoided him while straightening up the sage and decorations. He was watching her, scrutinizing everything she did.

"You should focus on the big fish," he said after a minute.

"The big fish," she repeated. She knew what he meant. The wealthy, the desperate, the ones who would pay anything for the chance to have one last conversation with a loved one. "I'm doing just fine, Dad."

"Not according to my—"

She faced him now. "You stay out of our books. Stay off my computer."

"It's not your computer. Who paid for it?"

"We needed it for the business."

"Yeah. Speaking of the business, what's your forecast for the next twelve months, fortune teller? Your sister, the brain, painted a bleak picture."

She didn't react. Of course, he was just testing her to see if she would confirm what he suspected—that House of Vale was failing, which it was—but it was really none of his concern.

"Ally wouldn't have said anything like that, Dad. You leave her alone."

"You forget this is my business, too."

"Not anymore."

He spoke in a lighter tone, as if to throw her off guard. "All I'm saying is you need to attract the clients who *really* matter."

"It's not that simple, Dad." She turned to face him. "People with a lot of money don't like to be seen in a place like this."

"You think I don't know that? How much are you spending on advertising?"

"Everything we can afford," she said.

"Obviously, that's not enough."

"Maybe we should rent out your apartment to a paying customer?"

His eyes narrowed. She'd gotten to him. "You'd like that, wouldn't you? To get rid of me. Don't forget I'm your father, and everything I do is for your own good. What else would you rather be doing?"

"Anything."

"Then leave."

"I can't."

"You won't," he said, "because it's all you know."

She closed her mouth. He was right. What else could she do after dropping out of high school and without a college degree? This was all she'd known all her life, and she was very good at it —a pro. Manipulating people was a skill she'd learned over the course of her life, and it had brought in a steady income, a home, her own business. She was living the American dream. Still, she couldn't help but feel there was something missing.

Ally came up beside them, and he inched back to let her squeeze by. He seemed to study her as she met his gaze.

"How many targets have you lined up for us today?" he asked sharply.

Ally didn't flinch. "Nobody in the queue yet. Just walk-ins."

Their father let out a laugh. "This place is a far cry from how it used to be."

"Nothing is like it used to be for you, Dad," Nora said.

He mumbled something and then turned away. His footsteps thumped down the hallway that led to his apartment at the back of the parlor. "Try not to mess anything up while I'm gone."

After the door clicked between them, she let out an exasperated sigh. "Thank you. He won't stay out of our way."

"He's in a good mood today," Ally said.

Nora let out a little laugh while arranging the tarot cards beside the black mirror, putting them into a neat little stack. "He hasn't had his pack of cigarettes yet."

Ally took a seat in the chair across from Nora where clients normally sat. She stretched out her arms across the table as if offering them. "How is he doing?"

Nora glanced down. She knew what Ally meant. Had the cancer spread, or were the treatments helping?

"He's improving. The doctor says he'll make a full recovery."

"That's good," Ally said.

"Yeah. It's just..."

Ally kept silent, waiting for her to finish.

Nora continued, "Who's going to pay all the bills? Dad's right. Things can't go on like this."

A moment later, the chime above the door rang, and Nora flinched. They both hurried out to the front office at the same time. A boy walked in, no older than ten years old, clutching a crumpled five-dollar bill.

"Hello?" His voice was small as he stepped inside apprehensively, with wide eyes.

Nora stepped toward him and crouched down to his level. "Can I help you?"

"I want to talk to Mommy." He held out the money.

Nora glanced at it, then toward the door. "Where's your mom?"

"She's in heaven."

For a moment, her Madame Lenora persona almost kicked in. She almost spoke to him in that same soothing voice she used for the wealthy clients who needed a little extra effort convincing them to part with their money. But there was something in the boy's eyes that stopped her. He had an innocence she hadn't seen in years. Gently pushing the money away, her theatrics faded.

"What's your name?"

"Jeffrey." He glanced back at the door. "Mommy died last week. Dad said I shouldn't come in here, but I want to talk to her."

The boy's father would come in at any moment. She hesitated, then reached out and put her hand on his shoulder. "Jeffrey, I don't need candles or special powers to tell you something important from your mother." She softened her voice even further. "Your mom loved you. And I know if she were here, she'd tell you to be strong and that she's proud of you."

The boy looked up and met her gaze. His eyes started to water. "Really?"

"Really."

The door burst open, and a man stormed in. He glared at

Nora and then down at the boy. "Jeffrey, I told you not to come in here."

Jeffrey shuddered and tried to hand the five-dollar bill to Nora. The man grabbed his arm and yanked him back while clutching the money. "What kind of scam are you running here? Ripping off kids now too? What's wrong with you?"

"I didn't—"

"Come on, Jeffrey." He dragged the boy out of the door. "Don't let me ever catch you near this place again."

The door slammed shut behind them. Glancing back at Ally, her sister had watched the confrontation from behind the front counter, and she gave a sympathetic smile.

"I'll get the table prepared for the next customer," Ally said.

Nora nodded. "Thanks. I'll put on my mask again."

❈ 3 ❈

Nora had just finished making a peanut butter and jelly sandwich for Lucy's school lunchbox when Daniel walked into the kitchen. He came around and kissed her on the back of the neck before taking a seat at the kitchen table. When she turned around, he was sorting through a pile of unpaid bills.

It was better to leave him alone. His morning smile was fading fast. She could see him out of the corner of her eye. He was watching her and tapping his fingers against the table. Her chest tightened. It was too early to have "a talk."

"Nora," Daniel said, "we have to figure this out."

"Not now." She rushed to finish packing Lucy's lunchbox, then snapped it shut with more force than necessary.

"When? After the bank forecloses on our house? After they shut off the electricity? We can't keep putting this off. We're running out of time."

She turned to face him. "Don't you think I worry about money, too? I see those bills every time I walk into this room."

Despite the rising tension, Daniel's expression was solemn. "Then let's do something about it."

"I *am* doing something about it." She forced herself to speak in a softer tone. "I'm working every day this week, even on Sunday. I'm trying."

Daniel watched her for a moment. "I see how hard you work, but maybe it's time you looked at a different career? Remember what we talked about? Lying to people isn't your true calling in life, anyway. You're taking advantage of them, selling them a fantasy."

Her face flushed warm. "If you didn't believe in my career, then why did you marry me?"

"I may not believe in what you do at that place, but I believe in *you*, Nora. I love you."

"I can't just walk away from everything. My clients depend on me."

"We depend on you too," he said. "That's what keeps me up at night. I've never doubted you—not once. It's just that I don't know how long we can keep going down this path."

"You're still trying to fix me."

Daniel shook his head slowly. "You're better than this."

She shrugged. "This is what I do, Daniel. You knew what you were getting into."

"I did, but I thought things would... evolve. Didn't we agree you would focus on something else after we got married? That you would move on?"

"It's not so easy."

"I'm sure it's not," Daniel said. "But it's not enough to support our family."

"It's more than the money, Daniel. My clients beg me for help. I give them closure."

"But it's not *real*," Daniel said softly.

Lucy hurried down the stairs a moment later, heading straight toward the front door. Her perfectly-brushed auburn hair bounced with every step.

"Lucy?" Nora said to her. "Did you finish all your homework?"

"Yes, Mommy." Lucy grabbed her jacket from the hook near the door and started to put it on.

Nora turned back to Daniel and lowered her voice. "Can we please talk about this later?"

"It's always later," he said softly. "Your family's business is important to you, but didn't we agree you would put all of that aside… eventually?"

"*Eventually*," she said, "I will. Just not today."

"Mommy?" Lucy called out while struggling with her jacket's zipper. "Are we going to see Aunt Ally and Grandpa Frank today?"

"No, honey," Nora answered. "I'll pick you up after school like normal and bring you home."

"I won't get to see Grandpa?"

"Not today, honey."

"That's another thing." Daniel turned away from Lucy and whispered, "He's been training her again."

Nora stepped closer to him. "I'm sure he just wants to pass down our family's traditions."

"He's trying to recruit her. The parlor is failing, so he's training Lucy behind our backs to step in if things fall apart with you. Is that what you want for her?"

Her face warmed again, but she forced herself to stay silent.

Daniel leaned back in his chair and crossed his arms. "It's time to move past your father's expectations. This is *our* family."

"You think I enjoy lying to my clients?" she said. "You think I want to live like this?" She made wide gestures toward the most obvious issues about their dated home. The broken table, the outdated appliances, the wallpaper they had never had the time to change since they moved in eight years earlier. So many repairs, so much unfinished or neglected.

"Can you please talk to him?" Daniel asked. "Tell him to stop teaching Lucy about the family business. I'm sure she'll eventually learn about it, to some degree, but she's only eight. I'm concerned about her mental health."

"He's not trying to hurt her."

"I'm not saying he is, but at her age... She doesn't need to hear about everything you do—talking with the dead, the Black Arts, and all that. Maybe you can find—"

"What?" She cut him off. "A *real* job? Is that what you were going to say? You know I don't have a college degree. I have *no other skills*. I can make minimum wage at any fast-food restaurant. Is that what you want? That's half of what I make now. How would we pay for everything then? Our food, our bills, my father's medical expenses? We may not be doing great, but at least it keeps us going."

"Barely."

"Tell me, what company out there pays a fair wage to someone with no degree, no real experience, and the word "psychic" on her résumé?"

Daniel glanced back at Lucy. "I just want to give her the life she deserves."

Nora followed his gaze. Lucy was watching them from the door, her hand clutching her backpack, her gaze jumping between them.

"Mommy," Lucy's small voice cut in. "I'm ready."

Nora forced a smile. "We'll leave in a minute." She turned back to Daniel, and then took another step toward him, pressing one hand against her heart. "This is my job, Daniel. It's my career. What else am I going to do?"

He stood with a sigh, scraping his chair against the floor. "There's got to be something."

"No," she said. "It's in my blood. I don't have a choice. If lying is the best way to pay the bills, then fine, I'll be the liar."

"You're *so* much better than that."

A silence hung between them, and at the same time the tension seemed to break between them like a storm finally passing. Nora sighed. "I'll think about it."

"That's all I ask."

His words hung in the air, and she took another deep breath

before walking over to join Lucy near the door. Nora slipped on her coat and gloves and glanced back at Daniel. He'd already turned back toward the pile of bills on the table with his face down.

Before opening the door, Lucy turned her angelic face up, her eyes showing a mix of fear and sadness. "I had another nightmare last night, Mommy."

Nora put her arms around Lucy's shoulders and nudged her forward. "Let's get you to school."

❧ 4 ☙

Nora walked into the parlor and headed straight to the back. From the sounds of rustling coming from the séance room, Ally was preparing everything for the next client. Instead of going in to talk with her, she continued down the short hallway leading into their father's apartment.

Stopping in front of his door, she took a deep breath. The distinctive smell of her father's menthol cigarettes sent a jolt of anxiety sweeping through her. At least he was awake, so why was she hesitating? What was she so afraid of?

The confrontation.

It was funny. Somehow, she had no problem with conjuring the dead for her clients, yet facing her father seemed the most daunting task in her life. Why?

Because her father was real.

Everything that happened in the séance room was just an illusion—a grand performance surrounded by velvet and candlelight. But her father loomed over every aspect of her life, haunting her mind, whispering in her ear, and steering her choices from the shadows. Even after so many years, his presence still shook her to the core. He was the one true ghost, the one she could never escape.

Reaching out to the doorknob, she hesitated, and then pulled her hand back. Any confrontation with him always turned out badly. Even when he was in a good mood, it turned on a dime if questioned about his intentions or ethics.

Despite the proximity to where she worked every day of the week, she rarely went inside his apartment at the back of the parlor. She only did so when it was absolutely necessary—once in a while to check in on him or if a delivery came and he needed it.

Taking a deep breath, she grabbed the doorknob again, turned it slowly, and pushed the door open. Nothing had changed from the previous visit, not even a little. It was still the same cramped, dim space. He hadn't cleaned anything and had stubbornly refused to accept her help. The walls were bare except for clusters of framed photos showing the parlor in its better days.

There were images of her father in his prime, grinning while holding up a Ouija board for the camera as if it were a prized possession. Her mother was standing next to him with a humble stance, resting one hand over her swollen belly. Was this photo taken when her mother had first gotten pregnant? Was that *her* in that belly? Her mother looked about the right age, although Ally had come along only two years later. Her mother had mentioned the first pregnancy once, that she'd almost lost the baby, and then had never mentioned it again. The thought sent a chill up her spine.

She'd almost died in the womb.

That was the hardest thing to see in this space—pictures of her mom. She had done the same thing for the business—a medium. She'd worked hard to keep it from crumbling beneath the weight of her father's incessant pressure to succeed.

Another framed photo showed her mother standing arm in arm with a group of friends. They were huddled around a massive stone slab with a flat top that resembled a table. The image was faded, probably taken during her college years judging by her big, teased hair, high-waisted jeans, and oversized earrings. They were outdoors somewhere, set against a stone background, although it was difficult to believe her mother had ever gone hiking.

Holding back her emotions, she stepped inside and glanced around the area. All the clutter made it difficult to focus on anything in particular. So many photographs and broken parlor props and supplies mixed in with all his discarded personal items.

Her father was sitting in his usual spot, a brown cloth recliner with the footrest permanently locked in the lower position because he'd broken it years earlier. He tapped the ash from his cigarette into the ashtray, then took another puff without looking back at her. His thinning gray hair was slicked back, and the lines on his face seemed a little deeper than the last time she'd stopped by. The television was blaring some reality TV show featuring large-breasted women with rich Hollywood lifestyles.

"Hey, Dad," she said.

He turned his head toward her and spoke in a gravelly voice, "Nora, are you looking for something? Money?"

"I'm just checking on you."

"Checking on me." He gave a little laugh. "Now I *know* you want something."

Stepping toward him but avoiding his gaze, she picked up a framed portrait of her and Ally in their younger years. It showed them wearing sparkly costumes, preparing to go on stage before a school play. She'd enjoyed performing back then, and it seemed like another life.

"I'm still alive," he said.

"Are you taking your medications?"

He snorted. "What's the point? It's obvious they're not doing any good." He gestured to the ashtray with his cigarette. "You here to lecture me about quitting again?"

She picked up a stray bottle from the coffee table and tossed it into a half-full trash can. "How are you feeling?"

"How do you think I'm feeling? Like hell, but that's not news to anyone, right?"

"I'm not here to lecture you about anything. Just wanted to see if you needed anything."

"What I need," he said, "is for you to stop pretending like you're the parent. I'm fine here. And I always will be fine here."

Nora turned back to him, forced a smile, and walked to the window. The blinds were shut, and she opened them without asking. "Lucy keeps having nightmares."

"Oh?" He took a puff from the cigarette.

"Maybe it's better not to talk to her about the business, at least for a few more years when she can process it better."

"It's a part of our heritage," he said. "She needs to understand that. Don't you want her to understand who you are, what we do for a living?"

"I do, but we think it's—"

"So this is an intervention," he interrupted.

She turned and faced him. "Please cut the drama. Nobody's doing an intervention on you." She folded her arms across her chest. "Just tone down the talk of the occult and communicating with the dead and all that with her. Can you do that?"

"Sure." He drew out the word long before taking another drag from his menthol cigarette. "I can do that."

"Good. I think that should help."

A silence stretched between them as she stared at the television until he finally spoke again. "How's it going up front today?"

"It's fine. Ally's keeping everything organized, a steady flow of customers."

"Alison. Oh yeah," Frank mumbled under his breath. "That girl is trouble. Too many opinions for her own good. College rotted her brain."

"She's doing a great job. Leave her alone."

"I'll leave her alone," he said, "but I can't stand the way she thinks she's smarter than the rest of us. A college degree means nothing in today's world. Are you going to let her run the show from now on?"

"She's not running the show," Nora said. "I need her help to keep things running smoothly. She's good at connecting with people."

He gave a dismissive wave of his hand. "She's dragging the place down. Help's one thing, but she never understood the family business. Why is she here?"

"I asked her to come back."

"There's your first mistake," he said. "When she left for college, things got better around here, but it started to fall apart again when she moved back. Let her go find a job as a pastor or whatever—"

"You don't even know what she studied."

"I do." He lifted his chin. "I paid her bills every month, didn't I?"

"She paid for most of it."

He scoffed. "A big waste of money."

"She earned a degree in comparative religion, and I'm jealous. At least *she's* trying to escape all this bullshit."

"Doesn't matter," he said. "She's an *intellectual* now."

"She's your daughter."

"And I'm her father, so where's the respect? Don't forget who built this place. Your mother and I worked our asses off to raise you kids."

"Don't start about Mom," Nora said. "I don't need a lecture."

"Alison's too soft with people. She doesn't know how to reel them in. I watch her sometimes, connecting with people, and she doesn't understand the game. The people who come in that door are customers. They're not here for a round of psychother-apy. They want a thrill, and we give it to them."

"I know how it works, Dad."

"Do you?" He narrowed his eyes. "Sometimes I wonder if your heart's still in it. You're getting soft these days too. I think Alison is talking you into—"

"Enough." Nora held up her hand, and her father scowled.

A silence filled the room until her dad rubbed out his cigarette in the ashtray. "I'm just your dad, so you can do what you want. It's your business now, but I want you to know that your mom and I sacrificed everything for you. We're lucky we had careers that kept us all together, something where we could work as a *family*. And then it sure as hell wasn't easy raising you on my own after she died. The parlor's kept this family above water when everything else failed. We did it all for you. Don't you understand that?"

Nora sank forward. She had heard his speech so many times she could recite it line by line, but this time he said it with too much melodrama. "And I'm supposed to feel good about that?"

Her father rolled his eyes. "You're missing the point."

"You're missing more than just the point, Dad. I didn't ask to be part of your schemes or..." She kicked aside a towel lying on the floor. "... to clean up your messes."

"I didn't ask you to come in here," he said.

Yes, so why *had* she gone in there? Why did she bother to pay his medical bills every month and listen to his nonsense week after week?

"You don't have to come in here anymore," he said in a soft voice, "if that's what you need. I'm fine with it, but we're a family, and family sticks together no matter what."

She nodded, but not in agreement, just to end the conversation. "I need to get back to work." She turned away from him and headed toward the door. "Just please don't mention anything else about the business to Lucy."

"You can't keep it from her forever."

"I can try."

"Sure," he said. "I won't say another word. Go do your thing out there and put on a good show. No matter what Alison tries to put in your brain, you're a natural, Nora. You've got the spark in you. Your mom and I saw that even when you were little. You were born to hustle."

She left his apartment and headed back to the parlor, but the weight of his words still hung heavy in her mind.

You're a natural, Nora. You were born to hustle.

5

Nora just wanted to get as far away from her father as possible. She hurried through the parlor toward the front door without speaking to Ally, without pausing, without grabbing her coat. The cool, minty smell of her father's cigarettes still clung to her clothes and filled her nostrils. Storming outside, she took a deep breath, closed her eyes against the morning light, and let the freezing air envelop her.

How long could she go on like this?

The biting air provided no answers. She shivered, folded her arms over her chest, and walked back inside. The little bell over the door jingled as it closed behind her.

Ally peeked her head out of the séance room and glanced around. "Was that you?"

"I needed to get a breath of fresh air."

Ally gave a knowing nod and headed toward the front desk. "I heard you come in and go to the back. How did it go?"

"As well as expected." Nora walked slowly toward Ally.

"You know," Ally said softly, "I overheard some people talking outside the Italian restaurant down the street. About this place. About you."

"Uh oh."

"Nothing bad. They sounded like they might stop by."

"You didn't get their info by any chance?"

"No time. I was on my way out, and they were on their way in. They sounded very interested. Believers."

"Let's hope they believe enough to stop by." Nora stepped over to the front desk. "Who's our first client?"

Ally handed her a card with notes. "Her name is Doreen."

Nora skimmed the notes. "Doreen," she repeated.

"She sounded nice," Ally said. "Sincere."

"Can't wait to meet her."

Ally gave her a curious look. "You're in early this morning."

"Yeah, I had to sort out some things with Dad. Better to do that in the morning so I have all day to calm down."

"If you need a break..."

Nora shook her head and then forced a smile, if only to let Ally know she wouldn't let her problems interfere with her job. "I have a good feeling about today."

"A good feeling?" Ally's eyebrows raised. "Are you planning to give a client some good news this time?"

"I always give them good news. It's better for business."

Ally grinned. "Smart."

"Did you do your research on her?" Nora asked.

Ally nodded. "I left a folder on your desk in the back."

"Anything interesting?"

"Just the usual. Her husband died several years ago, and she's overwhelmed with guilt, judging by the tone of her voice. She wants closure. I looked up her address on the internet. She's got a swanky house."

"How swanky?"

"A two-story on Lake Minnetonka. We should do well."

"Who else do we have coming in today?"

"Unfortunately... just her, plus the usual walk-ins."

"We can't keep things going on walk-ins. We'll have to spend more money on advertising or one of us will need to get out on the street corner and twirl one of those signs." She gave a wry grin.

Ally looked outside. "If it weren't so cold."

"I was just kidding," Nora said, "about twirling the sign."

"I'm not," Ally said. "I don't mind helping. As soon as it warms up, I can sit outside again and offer palm or astrology readings on the sidewalk like I did last summer. It's just a little slow right now because of the weather."

Nora stared out the storefront windows. The other businesses across the street were alive with customers despite the time of year. The sidewalk traffic this morning was even a little heavier than usual, but still, nobody came to her door. "I may join you this time."

"If I have to," Ally said, "whatever it takes."

Ally's quiet confidence warmed Nora's heart. Her little sister's tireless work ethic kept Nora from losing her mind on the worst days, something her father never understood. He saw Ally as a threat to their business, not a gift. But Ally was different. She didn't just know about occult practices, astrology, and palm reading—she lived it.

Nora frequently found Ally immersed in all the smelly old leather-bound books, something she would never have touched herself. Her sister was a walking archive of arcane knowledge, filling in the gaps when Nora stumbled, and it was a comfort having Ally there to talk the talk with clients in a way Nora never dared for fear of embarrassing herself. Even her sister's clothes walked the line between academic and arcane. She was wearing an earth-tone cardigan today, layered over a T-shirt with faded occult symbols as if she'd just stepped out of a forgotten library.

"It's a strange business, isn't it?" Nora asked. "Where do you see yourself in five years?"

This seemed to catch Ally off guard. "Hopefully... far from here—maybe somewhere warm—but I enjoy being surrounded by ghosts and the occult. You know I breathe this stuff."

"Is this place *that* exciting?"

"Not exactly *exciting*," she said, "but it has a certain allure."

Nora let out a little sigh. "Don't romanticize it. Remember, this is all just smoke and mirrors."

Ally held her gaze for a moment and then shrugged. "If you say so. It's not so bad, is it?"

"No, not *bad*. I mean, we *are* helping people. People will always need someone to help them through their grief. At the heart of it, that's exactly what we are, I guess. Grief counselors. I suspect we won't get rich off this anytime soon, but if they didn't come in here to help them through their pain, then they'd find someone else."

"You *are* helping them," Ally said with a nod. "I can see it on their faces on the way out."

"I just wish I could charge as much as a grief counselor. Maybe if we start a podcast or host midnight séances. Something to bring in the younger crowd."

"Maybe." Ally sat in a chair in front of the picture window and looked up at her. "I'll do a little research and see what the other parlors in town are doing. But you can't fake closure forever. One of these days, something real is going to come knocking."

Nora laughed. "If any of this were real, it would have come knocking a long time ago. Is that why you didn't argue when I asked you to come back? You're waiting to see a ghost?"

"It'll happen one of these days." Ally grinned. "I know you don't believe it, but there's a whole other side to reality. You think it's nonsense, because Mom and Dad never truly believed, but I know it's out there."

"Maybe Dad's right, Ally Cat," Nora laughed. "You *have* read too many books."

"Maybe." Ally smiled. "But there's always been something special about you, Nora."

Nora laughed. "That's ridiculous. You give me too much credit, but hold on to your superstitions, Ally, that's okay. It helps give the place some authenticity. You believe in me, in this place, and our clients sense that enthusiasm on a deeper level."

"Don't you believe *any* of it?" Ally asked.

Nora glanced back down the hallway toward her father's apartment. "I think I stopped believing in this place about the same time I stopped believing in Santa Claus."

"What about what you need, Nora? How long can you keep this up? Keep lying?"

Nora turned back and stared out across the street toward a flock of blackbirds that had gathered along the roof of a used bookstore. "According to Dad, until the day I die."

6

When the bell above the door jingled, both women fell silent. Nora hurried out to the front entrance, where a tall, elegant woman was glancing around the entrance with wide eyes.

Nora approached slowly and with an air of mystery. "Welcome, I'm Madame Lenora. How can I help you?"

The woman hesitated, scrutinizing the walls as if searching for hidden cameras. "This is a cozy little establishment."

"Intimacy is important in my profession. It creates a powerful connection to the other side. You must be Doreen."

"I am." They shook hands. The woman slipped off her white scarf and wool wrap coat, and hung them near the door.

"You're here just for the reading?"

Doreen nodded. "I'd like to talk about... I mean, *to* my husband, Robert."

"Absolutely." Nora gestured to the sign on the wall behind the countertop showing their prices and services. "How far would you like to take the experience?" The prices were listed from most expensive to least expensive. An immersive séance with a loved one was at the top and palm reading was at the bottom.

Judging by the woman's clothes, it wasn't difficult to guess which one she would choose.

"I'd like to take this as far as you can," Doreen said in a somber tone.

"Of course, we can do that," Nora said.

Ally came around from behind the counter and shook the woman's hand. "I'm Ally. You spoke with me on the phone?"

"Yes, thank you so much for explaining the process so well. I wasn't sure if this was the right thing to do. You know, I've never done anything like this before." The woman glanced back toward the door. "It's not…"

"Don't you worry about a thing," Nora said. "Privacy is a priority here. We get a lot of first-time clients."

Ally gestured toward the hallway. "When you're ready, I'll be happy to take you to the séance room."

Doreen nodded once and lifted her chin. "I'm ready now."

Ally led them into the séance room with Nora trailing a few steps behind. She scanned Doreen's appearance for last-minute clues about her social class, habits, even her diet—anything that she could use to enhance her performance.

Gathering in the room, Doreen paused just inside the doorway and glanced across the dim space. "Will there be a light on during the séance?"

"Only candlelight," Nora said smoothly, "but there's nothing to fear in this room. Darkness and isolation help us better connect with the spirit world. Is there anything in particular you'd like to ask your husband?"

"I've made a list." Doreen clutched her purse a little tighter but offered no further details.

Nora nodded and gestured toward the chair across the table. "Please have a seat and, when you're ready, tell me about Robert."

After the woman had settled into her seat, Nora moved into position opposite her, making sweeping motions around the room. Ally slipped out of the room during that time. Her sister would make her way into the control room within moments, watching every interaction behind the one-way mirror. They could communicate wirelessly through the obsidian mirror resting on the table. Ally had rigged the object, burying a small LED screen just below its surface, which allowed the faintest amount of light to pass through—enough light to pass along words, symbols, and even pictures to aid Nora in her "abilities."

The old woman's trembling hands clutched at her purse. "We were married for almost twenty-five years when he passed away suddenly." She stared down at the items on the table but looked up sharply at Nora. "Should I tell you *everything*? Maybe it's better..."

Nora tilted her head. "Tell me anything you want. We'll speak with your husband soon enough."

"Of course, yes." Doreen took a deep breath. "Robert died of a heart attack a few months before our twenty-fifth anniversary. Such a shame. We'd been planning the thing for years—what we would do, who we would invite. And he passed away so suddenly." A weight came over her face. "I just need to know he's okay, that he forgives me."

Nora began her usual process by lighting the sage on the table between them and then putting it on the shelf behind her. Each practiced step was to showcase Nora's confidence with all aspects of the occult. She nudged the obsidian mirror toward her, running her fingers along the edges with a bit of flair. "Why do you feel you need his forgiveness?"

Doreen looked down. "Oh, I was horrible to him the morning he died. We argued about something, something so incredibly stupid. But it's always the little things, isn't it? The little things that don't matter in the end. He wanted to change our plans and take a trip overseas alone for our anniversary— something more intimate—instead of spending it with our families. I wanted to be with family and share our special moment with them here, but he didn't see it that way. That's all. Such a simple disagreement, but we argued *so much* about it, as silly as it sounds. Family and friends are important to me. Better than rushing around with a bunch of strangers and tour guides and vendors trying to sell you happiness. Don't you think?"

Nora swallowed and nodded. "Of course."

Doreen continued, "He wasn't happy when I left him that morning to go to work. Neither of us was happy. So we didn't talk when he came home for the longest time. But when I entered the bedroom to tell him I had already decided to give him the grand vacation he wanted, it was too late. He was already gone, and I never got to say goodbye. I never got to say I'm sorry."

Nora's thoughts jumped back to her own mother's death a few years earlier, and her sudden departure from this world from a heart attack. She too hadn't gotten the chance to say goodbye. A surge of emotional pain swept through her, but Nora pushed it away quickly and spoke in a soothing voice, "I'm very sorry to hear of your husband's death. Let's see if we can find him."

Doreen nodded, and Nora stretched her hands out across the table. The woman seemed to pick up on the cue and did the same, grabbing her hands in the middle with the obsidian mirror and candle between them.

Closing her eyes, Nora began her usual performance, leaving her eyes cracked open just a bit to watch her client's expressions. The light from the candles on the table danced across the woman's face, and she paused for a long moment before finally whispering Robert's name. "Robert, can you hear me?"

Doreen's hands twitched.

"Robert," Nora repeated, "I have Doreen here with me. She wants to visit with you in her time of despair in order to heal her heart."

Doreen's eyes were partially closed, but they grew wider as Nora tightened her grip on the woman's fingers.

"Yes," Nora said. "I can see Robert's spirit in the distance. He's aware of your pain. Would you like to talk to him?"

"Yes," Doreen said with a little gasp of breath. "Of course. Please let me talk to him."

"Robert," Nora said again. "Please join us in this space so your wife can find closure. Her heart aches for your presence. Please stand here beside us and speak through me, so I can fill the void in her soul."

The room grew a little colder. Right on cue. Ally was doing her job perfectly behind the mirror. The lights and sounds would start as soon as Nora spoke a few trigger words.

"Robert is coming closer now," Nora said. "I feel he also wants to speak with you. He holds strong feelings about his last moments, things he wants to share."

"Yes," Doreen said with excitement and longing. "I would love to talk with you again, Robert."

"He's been waiting for you, too."

"Can you hear me, Robert?" Doreen pleaded to the air around them.

"He is here!" Nora rolled her eyes up, letting her eyelids flitter. "Speak with him now."

"I should have done this sooner," Doreen scolded herself. Tears had started flowing down her cheeks. The clients always broke down at this stage of the séance, and sometimes Nora would need to pause for them to recover from the sudden burst of emotions before continuing, but Doreen was holding up well... so far. "Does he forgive me? Please tell me he forgives me. I'm so sorry, Robert."

"Robert," Nora said, "Doreen is heartbroken and needs your forgiveness. She is sorry for the way she acted before you died. Do you—"

Another burst of cold air rushed into the room, this time blowing out the candle and sending a chill through Nora's chest. She shivered, although she kept her eyes closed.

Doreen gasped. "Is that him? Robert, please forgive me!"

"He hears you," Nora said. The sounds and visuals would

begin shortly, but the extra burst of cold air was unexpected. Still, Nora continued, "He says, 'I forgive you.'"

"Oh, I'm so sorry, my sweetheart." Doreen squeezed Nora's hands with more force than Nora had thought possible from the woman's thin fingers. "I've missed you every day since you left me. I was so selfish to leave you alone after our argument. If only I had been there to save you."

"Don't blame yourself," Nora said in a low voice, as if emulating Robert's voice. "I forgive you. Please take care of our children—" Nora hesitated. Had Ally's notes indicated Doreen even had children? The details were jumbled now, maybe confusing it with a different client.

"Yes, the children!" Doreen seemed to brighten. "Our two cats, Benny and Bela. Our only children."

Nora focused on the candle, but her vision blurred. Something was wrong. Still, she continued, "Please forgive me for leaving you so soon."

"I do," Doreen said. "Oh, I do."

"We should have celebrated our anniversary at home, like you wanted."

"It doesn't matter anymore, my love," Doreen said. "I miss you so much. Everything is so pointless since you left me. What should I do?"

Nora's head ached. The room seemed to spin. Worse than any hangover. She opened her mouth to speak again when a loud crash came from somewhere near the entrance to the parlor. A sudden gust of cold air twisted its way across the table. At the same time, she blacked out.

❧　7　☙

She awoke disoriented and terrified, her face and chest pressed against the table. Sitting upright again, the darkness seemed to stretch out infinitely in every direction. Her temples throbbed with pain, and she tried to focus on anything within the darkness. Was she alone? Had she awakened from a dream?

Her senses came back slowly.

Doreen's voice jarred her back to reality. "What's happening?"

The table's velvet cloth grounded her to the reality of the séance room. In the dim light, Nora could see that Doreen was still in her seat, but the woman's face was full of panic.

The séance.

"It's okay," Nora slurred as she regained her awareness and sat up.

Where is Ally? She hasn't started the visuals yet.

"I think I passed out," Nora said. "We should continue."

"Of course," Doreen said into the darkness, glancing around frantically. "Is he still here? Is Robert angry with me?"

Nora's heart beat faster as she waited for Ally to do something—anything—to help calm the woman down. *Dammit.*

Hurry, Ally. Switch on a light, create a noise, just please break the tension.

Another deafening crash filled the air, but this time it came from the other side of the room, only a few feet away. Something made of glass had hit the floor and shattered. Doreen cried out and shifted her chair away from the table. Had Ally dropped one of the props? If so, it wasn't planned. Still, Nora had to continue. She couldn't let the woman leave. Not yet. She needed the money, and they'd barely begun.

"Sometimes... spirits have trouble manifesting," Nora said, trying to regain control of the situation.

A familiar soft glow came from a large crystal on the shelf beside the sage, rigged to light up in an almost imperceptible way. Ally had finally stepped in with the theatrics, but judging by the way Doreen's eyes darted around the room, maybe it was already too late.

"What does he want from me? I'd like to continue speaking with him."

Nora nodded. "He forgives you."

Doreen pointed nervously at the shattered glass across the floor. "Then why did he break that?"

Nora still couldn't focus well enough to see the object that had fallen but followed the woman's gaze to the floor. A crystal? A mirror? Ally had placed so many objects on the shelves around them it was impossible to know for sure without switching on the lights again.

"He forgives you," Nora repeated without thinking.

Another object rattled on a shelf further up and then plummeted to the floor, breaking into pieces. None of this was scripted.

How had Ally broken the items?

And... *why?*

Things had been going well until...

She'd blacked out. It had never happened before.

Something moved in the room. Something shifted in the cool

air. A presence. Something shadowy yet hollow, it occupied the space only a few feet away. The sound of footsteps moved closer, emerging from the darkest corner of the room where the items had fallen from the shelf. Something crunched across the shattered glass toward them, and the air grew even colder. Had Ally cranked up the air conditioner? Nora shivered in the icy chill.

"Why is he doing this?" Doreen pleaded. "Robert! Why are you doing this to me? I'm so sorry."

"It's okay," Nora said, her head still reeling from blacking out. "He forgives you, I promise."

Doreen stared toward the presence, then stood sharply. "He... I feel... he's very angry with me. I don't feel good about this at all. Is he angry with me?"

Nora also stood and reached out to the woman, gesturing to the chair. "Please stay in your seat. He has more to say."

Doreen shook her head. "He doesn't forgive me."

"I swear it. He does."

"No." The woman scrambled toward the door with tears flowing down her cheeks. Bits of shattered glass crunched beneath her shoes. She fumbled with the doorknob before throwing the door open and rushing out into the hallway.

Light poured in, and the full extent of the damage became clear. Not just any vase had fallen from the shelf, but her mother's handmade clay vase, fired with some of her grandmother's ashes mixed in. The one her mother had gifted to her on her wedding day.

Nora's heart sank. The pieces lay scattered across the floor in every direction. Everything was broken beyond repair. Even worse, Doreen had stepped through the ashes on her dash out the door, leaving a dusty trail of footprints behind her.

Turning back toward the darkened corner where she'd heard the footsteps, she saw nothing. No explanation for how the objects had fallen from the shelf while other objects still sat right beside it undisturbed. No explanation for the footsteps or the strange presence. No explanation for any of it.

Had Ally installed new effects without telling her? Ally *had* planted new speakers in every corner of the room to give a surround sound effect. But could Ally have created such a convincing trick as the footsteps crunching over glass? It was too perfect. Too *real*.

Nora hurried after the woman, catching up with her near the entrance, just as Doreen was putting on her coat. But before Nora could say a word, she choked in a breath.

A patch of blood was smeared against the outside of the main parlor window. Fresh blood, still oozing down the glass, carried bits of black feathers with it.

This was the crash she'd heard from the séance room.

Doreen let out a scream while Nora rushed forward. A dead blackbird lay motionless on the sidewalk just outside the window, its broken neck twisted unnaturally against a mangled wing.

While staring down at it, another blackbird swooped in and crashed against the glass inches from Nora's face. The jarring force hit the glass as if someone had tried to put their fist through it.

More blood. More feathers.

She stumbled back.

At least the glass held.

Glancing toward the sky, an entire flock of blackbirds was circling overhead. They were flying low in a narrow vortex as if caught in a tornado. One by one, they broke away from the flock, swooping in like black arrows toward the window. Not the window. Toward *her*.

Another wet thump shook the glass, followed by another, and then another. The sickening sounds grew louder and more frequent. Nora and Doreen backed away at the same time.

Moments later, the swarm of birds hit the window all at once.

This time, it shattered.

Nora covered her face while Doreen turned away and

crouched forward as glass exploded across the floor and the birds flooded inside.

Chaos filled the parlor.

The deafening sound of screeching birds drowned out any cries for help. Many of the birds died instantly. Others writhed helplessly on the floor, their wings mangled, their feathers ripped off, torn apart by the shards of glass still clinging to the edges of the window.

A few of them trudged out of the mess toward her, their black eyes wide and hungry. Their bloodied feathers twitched as they thrashed across the floor before finally collapsing and falling silent like the others.

Nora pulled on Doreen's coat to move her back, but the woman pushed toward the exit instead and fled the shop. The bell jingled violently as she slammed the door on her way out.

Centered within all the gore and glass, one of them stood out. The largest one, lying motionless on the floor, blood still dripping from its glossy black eyes. It seemed to focus its gaze on her accusingly.

Ally rushed out of the back room a moment later and gasped as she joined Nora's side. "Oh, my God."

Nora held back her tears. "Can anything else go wrong today?"

Ally shivered in the freezing air that swept in around them. "I told you one day something real would come knocking."

8

Nora found a plastic tarp in the back storage closet to temporarily patch up the broken window. But even after sealing the edges with duct tape, the cool air still leaked in. A few loose papers and dried herbs rustled across the front desk.

On top of everything, the smell of dead birds hung in the air, with blood smeared across the tile floor and shards of glass shimmering in every direction. It wasn't just the dead birds or the glass that bothered her. It was what Ally had said that kept popping into her mind.

Something real *had* come knocking.

"This is insane." Ally used a small broom and dustpan to sweep up the glass. She was doing a great job keeping things under control, but the strain was clear in her voice.

Nora's gaze stopped on the largest bird on the floor, its bloody feathers mixed in with all the glass. The bird lay motionless but seemed to stare directly at her. Had it known what it was doing when it crashed through the window? Racing toward something inside their parlor... or trying to escape from something outside?

Ally seemed to read her thoughts and asked, "Why do you think they did this?"

"Why?" Nora said. "The birds get disoriented. They don't see the glass and fly into it head-on."

"But they usually don't break through the glass, right?" Ally said. "And why... so many?"

Nora looked at her wryly. "Are you suggesting they tried to commit suicide?"

Ally grinned. "Not saying that, but it *is* a bit strange. Don't you think?"

Nora ran her fingers through her hair and let out a sharp breath.

A moment later, a familiar grating voice filled the air. "What the hell is going on out here?"

Nora winced. Her father stepped into the front parlor, moving a little slower than usual but with the same entitled presence. His hair was a mess now, and his shirt was unbuttoned halfway down. He lifted a lit cigarette to his mouth and took a drag, blowing the smoke out with unusual force. He didn't look concerned. He looked annoyed.

"We had an accident," Nora said coldly. She didn't like the way he was looking over the mess as if it were somehow their fault.

He cringed. "Holy shit, are you running a séance parlor or a goddamn slaughterhouse?"

Ally continued cleaning up the glass without pausing, although she straightened a bit when their father came into the area.

"We've got it under control," Nora said.

He gestured toward the window. "You're going to need a hell of a lot more duct tape than that to fix this mess. The wind'll rip right through that."

"Thanks for the insight, Dad." Nora moved toward Ally and studied the broken window again. Despite his annoying tone, he was right. She grabbed another plastic tarp and stepped up onto the ladder beside the opening. Ally helped to hold it up as they worked together, adding another layer of duct tape over what they had already done.

He snorted as if he had won some battle. "You better call someone right away to fix it—today—or do you plan on leaving it open to break-ins?" He gestured to the mess as cigarette smoke streamed around the room driven by the gusts of air seeping in through the unpatched cracks. "You won't get any customers walking through that door when it looks like you pissed off a demon."

"We won't leave it like this." Nora carefully smoothed out the tarp near the bottom edge of the hole and spoke directly to her sister. "Ally, can you hold this while I add the tape?"

"Sure." Ally stepped over and held it down while Nora taped it again and again, intentionally ripping the tape from the spool louder than necessary to drown out everything her father was mumbling. "We'll fix what we can now, and I'll get someone in here to repair the glass as soon as I can."

"This is a disaster," he said.

"We know, Dad," Ally said.

Nora didn't want to hear his voice anymore, but again, he was right. It *was* a disaster. Walk-in customers were a vital part of their business, and now things were worse. Much worse. The weight of everything crashed down on her all at once. How much would someone charge to replace the glass? Hundreds? Thousands? Would insurance cover some of it? Either way, it was certainly going to cost too much.

She finished and then backed away with her teeth clenched, keeping her back toward her father. Ally must have noticed the tension on her face because she spoke in a light tone and touched Nora's shoulder while passing by.

"Well, I'm going to look at this as a sign of good luck," Ally said.

"Good luck?" her father scoffed. "What have you been smoking?"

Ally shrugged, then returned to cleaning up the glass. "It's an omen, right? Death, transformation. Blackbirds are a sign that things are about to change."

"For the better, I hope," Nora said.

"That's bullshit," her father said. "The only *sign* that broken window conveys is a sign of failure. Right now, it's just screaming to the customers, 'Keep walking!'"

She stared at the mess for a long moment, if only to avoid his condescending stare. The pressure weighed on her mind, but she needed to do something.

"We're going to close up for today," she said, brushing past her father without looking at him. "At least until we get this fixed."

Her father scoffed. "Oh yeah? You're going to give up just like that? How much money do you have stashed away that I don't know about? The place stays open. Get out there, walk the streets, sell palm reading to the people on the sidewalk like you used to."

"It's twenty degrees outside, Dad."

"Doesn't matter. Tough times require tough measures. Get out there and work for your money. Hand out leaflets."

"We don't have any leaflets." She stopped and glared at him. "All the marketing is done online nowadays." He stared back, but she didn't look away. "Instead of complaining, why don't *you* get out there and drum up some business like *you* used to? Or grab a broom and help us clean up this mess instead of pissing me off."

"This isn't our fault," Ally added.

"Never said it was." He took another long drag of his cigarette and shrugged. "It's your business. Do what you want." Without another word, he turned away and headed back to his apartment.

Nora waited until the door at the end of the hallway clicked shut before she let out a long, slow breath and waved her hand through the air. The cigarette smoke still lingered.

"You okay?" Ally asked.

"I'm fine," she lied. Walking to the front door, she flipped over the 'CLOSED' sign on the hook.

Only a short time later, the area was clean enough that they could step across the floor without sliding over glass. Nora stepped back and glanced around. "It'll do for now." She turned to Ally and frowned. "Dad's right. Nobody will step in here until it gets repaired."

"Are you sure you don't want me to stay?" Ally asked. "There's still broken pieces on the floor in the séance room."

Nora shook her head and gave a warm smile. "I'll take care of it. You deserve a little free time."

Ally gave her one last look, then nodded and walked toward the back exit, grabbing her bag from behind the front desk on the way out.

Nora followed her. "I'm—"

A loud knock came from the front door. They paused and looked at each other with wide eyes. She hadn't turned off the front lights yet, but it was hard to believe anyone would approach their parlor in such a ragged condition.

Another knock came louder, and the sound echoed through the parlor.

❧ 9 ❧

Nora cautiously stepped out into the front room, while Ally hurried ahead of her toward the door without slowing down. They paused together a few feet from the door. It was a man in a hooded parka, but the "CLOSED" sign on the door obscured his face.

Ally peeked around the edge of the sign before reaching for the door handle. "Should I let him in?"

"What have we got to lose?"

Ally opened the door, and an elderly man greeted them with a sympathetic smile. A burst of cold air rushed in around him.

He looked like a college professor or a librarian—someone who'd read a lot of books in his life—judging by his silver hair, thick black glasses, and a gray scarf wrapped around his neck. His cheeks were bright red, and he shivered while glancing around at the mess on the floor. "Are you okay?" he asked. "I saw what happened with the birds, but I couldn't make it over here until now."

Nora inched toward Ally but relaxed a bit. They'd cleaned up the glass and birds, but the sickening smell still hung in the air. Ally had mopped the area once, but it would need another pass.

"It caught us off guard," Nora said.

"I'm sure it did." He glanced back, looking toward the sky. "I've never seen anything like that. They came from across the street—a whole flock of them—and swooped down all at the same time like something startled them."

"Nobody got hurt." Nora glanced down at the remnants of glass lodged in the corner near the door.

"Glad to hear it," he said. "Strangest thing I've ever seen."

A gust of icy wind swept in through the open door. "Would you like to come in?" Ally asked, opening the door a little wider.

He glanced around the front room curiously. "Maybe now isn't a good time."

"Come in." Nora shivered.

He nodded. "Thank you."

She shut the door behind him.

While slipping off his scarf, he glanced around the parlor again with a sharpened intensity. "Bad time to break a window."

Nora moaned. "I was just about to call someone to fix it."

"That's why I stopped by," he said. "Thought I might help."

Nora glanced at her feeble patchwork over the window and then down at his clothes. "Do you fix windows?"

"Never tried," he said with a smile. "But I know a few people who do."

He's a salesman.

Nora lost her smile. "We'll need to get an estimate first."

"No pressure," he said, extending his hand. "You must be Nora."

"That's me." She shook it and narrowed her eyes at him. "Have we met before?"

He shook his head. "No, but I've always thought of stopping by to check out this place."

"You've heard of me?"

He nodded politely. "I'm familiar with your family and what you do here."

Nora broadened her smile. "We take our work seriously.

Since you're here... any chance we could interest you in a reading? Maybe barter our services to get the window repaired?"

He pressed his lips together and then tilted his head. "I wasn't... I'm not sure I'm interested in—"

"It wouldn't take long." Nora moved toward the counter, gesturing toward the list of services and their prices.

"That's a tempting offer." He looked at her for a long moment with a growing grin. "But I'm not sure how my parishioners would react."

Nora gasped. "You're a priest?"

He held out his hand and spoke in a casual tone, "Father Antonio de la Cruz. Please call me Father Tony. Does that bother you?"

"No... It's just that priests don't usually stop by here."

"That doesn't surprise me. I normally wouldn't have, but for the unusual circumstances." He glanced back out through the broken window, turning his curious gaze toward the sky. "Very unusual."

"Maybe they were escaping from something—a predator— looking for a place to hide."

"Possibly," he said. "They sure came out of nowhere. Maybe the cold disoriented them. Most of the birds have flown south by now, but there's always some that stick around a little longer than they should. They might have seen their reflection in the glass, and that's what confused them." He turned back to them and straightened. "The important thing is everyone is okay."

"We're fine," Nora said. "Just... a bit rattled."

"A few years ago," he said, "I had a whole family of sparrows crash into the rectory window. Sounded like the world was ending."

Nora gave a small laugh. "It's hard to understand how something like this can happen."

He glanced back toward the front desk, then down the hallway leading toward their father's apartment. "That... that's just as I remember it."

"You've been here before?"

"Many years ago. Just after I became a priest." He grinned. "So, you can count the decades and take your best guess."

"What brought you back then?" Ally asked.

"Sheer curiosity," he said. "I'd never stepped inside a place like this, and I wanted to meet your parents after hearing about them for years. The Church took a more judgmental stance back then, with the rise of everything occult. It became quite popular in the '80s—almost glamorous. Devil worship and demons made a big splash in the media through books and movies. Everyone feared it was the end of times. And witnessing what I did today, it seems those fears may have returned."

"I'm sure you don't think this has anything to do with the end times," Nora said.

He smiled and his face softened. "No, of course not. Forgive me. I'm only drawing crude comparisons. Just thinking out loud. When you've seen as much as I have, it's impossible not to make the connections. I'll have someone from the church call you about your window as soon as I get back to my office. I'm sure someone can stop by to help you this afternoon."

Ally cleared her throat. "How much will that cost?"

He shook his head. "No cost. Under the circumstances, the repair is free. I have a lot of friends in high places, don't you know?" He winked.

Nora's brow went up. "Thank you."

He waved it off. "No worries, but let me ask you something. Has anything like this happened here before?"

"First time, and hopefully the last," Nora said.

"Why?" Ally asked, leaning forward curiously.

"It's just so... remarkable. The way they all dropped at the same time. Like a riotous mob."

"You think they targeted us?" Nora asked.

"I doubt that very much," Father Tony said. "But please contact me if you have any other concerns."

"What kind of concerns?" Ally asked.

"If you notice anything unusual," he said. "I'm sure you've encountered your fair share of strange situations over the years with your clients."

"Nothing we couldn't handle," Ally said.

"I expect that's true," he said with a small nod. "Your family has had a long time to develop its gifts. But do be careful—grief is a fragile thing. Sometimes, it's better left in the hands of someone trained to bear the weight of it."

"I would call myself a professional," Nora said.

"Of course," he said quickly, lifting a hand in apology. "I didn't mean to insult you. It's just... emotions are delicate. They can be nudged into dangerous places if pushed too far."

Nora swallowed. "I help people. I give them closure."

"I believe you do," he said gently. "But closure can't be forced. You can't summon what isn't there. You can only invite into this world what's already waiting to be found."

"Is that what you believe?"

"It's not a matter of belief," he said softly. "It's the truth."

A silence fell between them until Ally spoke up. "We should probably finish cleaning."

"Yes," he said. "I'm sorry for keeping you."

"Thank you for checking on us," Ally said.

He pushed his lips together and gave a solemn nod before turning back toward the door. "I'm always available to help. Even though we may stand on opposite sides of the ideological scale, we're allies in more ways than you think. I've seen the kindest people lose themselves chasing answers that weren't meant to be found. It's heartbreaking, really. If you ever need someone to talk to about anything at all, my door is always open. St. Michael's Catholic Church."

Another wave of cold air rushed in through the broken window, and Nora shivered. "Thank you."

He left a moment later, and as soon as the door closed behind him, the weight of everything churned her stomach.

✻   10   ✻

After Father Tony left, Nora walked back into the séance room and sat at the table for several minutes with her arms crossed tightly over her chest. The chaos in the front parlor left her feeling heavy and confused.

What the hell had happened out there? Her sister had suggested that the incident with the blackbirds was a sign of good luck, a transformation—an omen for change.

Bullshit.

Everything had changed, all right, but nothing suggested good luck. The disturbing images flashed through her mind—the twisted shadows in the séance room with Doreen, the sickening thump of the blackbirds crashing into the glass, and their bloody carcasses littering the parlor floor, their wings still fluttering frantically in the throes of death.

Nothing lucky about that.

Ally came in a short time later and stood motionless in the doorway. "So, are we going to talk about what just happened?"

"Which part?" Nora scoffed. "The stuff with Doreen, the blackbirds, or what Father Tony said?"

Ally stepped into the room, glanced back down the hall

toward their father's apartment, then closed the door behind her. "All of it."

"How can you suggest what happened with the birds was 'good luck'?" She gestured at the bell on the table. "And that— Did you see what happened with that thing?"

Ally stepped closer. "It went off on its own."

"We have to get a new one," Nora said. "That one's obviously faulty."

Ally's dark eyes narrowed. "Come on, Nora. You know there's no electronics in the bell. No way for it to go off like that when it's on the table, and... I saw what you were looking at over in the corner at the shadows." Ally leaned against the table, tracing her fingers along the edge of the polished wood. "What did you see?"

Nora sat up and looked at her sister with an amused expression. "I didn't see anything."

"You had a strange look in your eyes," Ally said.

Nora rolled her eyes and leaned away from her. "What I saw doesn't matter. None of this proves anything, if that's what you're implying here. What matters is that suddenly I feel like I'm losing my mind, so if you're suggesting I actually summoned a spirit..."

Ally shrugged. "It's possible. They come through like that, with little signs and manifestations."

"Ally," Nora scoffed, "please don't start with all that mystical mumbo-jumbo just because you've read a few old books."

Ally growled with her mouth closed, a little thing she did to express her displeasure once in a while. "It's not just mumbo-jumbo. I've spent years in college studying this stuff. Forget all the stuff Mom and Dad taught us about presenting a good experience for the client. This stuff is *real*. Please don't underestimate the experience we just had."

Nora looked at her for a long moment. "We both got taught the same stuff, the same indoctrination, so I can appreciate where you're coming from, but we didn't have *an experience*."

"You think I don't recognize the real shit when I see it?" Ally asked. "It's not just from reading books. I've seen *plenty* over the years, and not just from watching YouTube videos. I've interviewed countless mediums and those who practice folk magic, watched hundreds of rituals happen *right in front of me,* including communication with the dead around the country. There are plenty of things I've seen that I can't explain. There's a skill in listening to the things people like you ignore."

"People like me? You mean frauds."

"I didn't mean it like that. I meant skeptics."

"If you know so much—" Nora pushed her chair back and stood up, then stepped away from the table. "—why don't you sit in here and give it a shot?"

"I can't," Ally said. "You know I can't. And I'm not trying to upset you. Believe me, I wish I could do what you're doing, just on a more authentic level. But I also didn't come back here after college to watch you follow the same path as Mom and Dad. You've got a way with people, even if it's not entirely honest. You've got a heart, believe it or not, and a wonderful gift. When you stop pretending and start listening to the clients, then you'll work some real magic. Maybe even just listen to me once in a while?"

Nora looked away and spoke just above a whisper. "So you're saying I just conjured a real spirit?"

"Maybe," Ally said simply. "What did you see in the shadows? A figure? A face? You can't keep lying to yourself."

Nora dropped into her chair again. "That wasn't anything. Maybe just the candles flickering, reflecting off the mirror. If anything I ever did in here is real, then... if what I saw just now is real, then why now? I've been doing this for years without anything unusual happening."

Ally took another step forward. "We can take a look at that, but this is something you need to take seriously. We need to find out what really happened here just now. Together."

Nora looked over into the corner where the shadows had moved earlier. She *had* seen something odd, but nothing that couldn't be explained. She lifted the bell off the table, turned it upside down, shook it, ringing it a few times before placing it down again. The bell ringing on its own had no rational explanation, but still, she refused to join Ally's train of thought.

"You didn't have anything to do with this?"

Ally shook her head. "No."

"Seriously?"

"Seriously."

Nora gazed at the velvet cloth draped across the table and all the trinkets she'd carefully laid out around the room. Many of the items were passed along from her mother and father's business. All traces of shadows had disappeared.

She looked up and stared into her sister's eyes. "You didn't do anything to cause the shadows?"

Her sister showed a pained expression. "I'm not lying, and I wouldn't do anything to sabotage your session. I would *never* lie to you, even though we're surrounded by all this fake shit."

Nora swallowed. Why had she doubted her sister even for a moment? "I don't know. It's just hard to believe in any of this after watching Mom and Dad's nonsense our whole lives. It's just a way to make a living, you know?"

"It's more than that," Ally said.

"No," Nora said. "It's not."

"One day, you'll see what I mean."

"Listen," Nora said, "I know you're the one who believes in all this stuff, but maybe you're just taking this a little too seriously. Maybe you just want to prove a point and make me see things your way."

Ally narrowed her eyes, then spoke in a trembling voice, "If I wanted to prove a point, I wouldn't stoop to your level. How can you even say that? I've stood by you even when I didn't agree with what you're doing because I believed in you, that somewhere in all this deception, we *are* doing something good for people deep down. Am I wrong?"

Ally's wise words hit Nora like a dagger.

Her sister continued, "You're so afraid of what this means that you're willing to blame me instead of facing the truth." Ally shook her head. "You're finally experiencing something real in your life, Nora. You can't just pretend it doesn't exist. Something *real* just happened here today. Something you did brought it here."

Nora dropped her head into her hands and ran her fingers through her hair. "Everything is falling apart."

"No, just you." Ally turned and walked out of the room.

Nora sat alone at the séance table for a long time. She closed her eyes and tried to clear her mind. The room was starting to warm up again. Still, she shivered within the stillness.

She shook her head. "I don't know what to believe."

A faint whisper passed through the air. "Believe."

$\approx$ 11 $\approx$

Nora stepped inside her house and hung her keys on the hook by the door. Coming home should have been the best part of her day. Lucy's soft voice came from somewhere just out of sight, and the smell of garlic came from the kitchen. Daniel was cooking dinner. It was everything she valued in life, and the tension should have stopped at the front door. Instead, it seemed to magnify the chaos swirling in her mind.

She'd called him earlier, telling him about what had happened with the birds while Father Tony's window repair buddies were replacing the store glass. But she'd said nothing about all the other bizarre experiences: the bell and the shadows in the séance room, and the whisper after Ally had stepped away.

Believe.

The word echoed through her mind. She couldn't shake it.

Daniel glanced over when she came in, while taking a pan of garlic bread out of the oven. He smiled warmly for a moment, but then it faded, probably mirroring the stress on her own face. "We'll get through this."

She removed her coat and hung it near the door.

"Mommy!" Lucy cried out. Her infectious energy seemed to come out of nowhere.

Nora turned to face her daughter's sweet face staring up at her. There were bits of food clinging to her sweatshirt, and her hair was a mess. She threw her little arms around Nora's waist.

"Hi, sweetheart." She kneeled and embraced Lucy, forcing the smile at first, but then it expanded as Lucy's enthusiasm warmed her heart. This was why she worked so hard. This was why she struggled through each day, lowering herself to pay the bills with the only skills she seemed to possess. Deception.

"Look what I made in art class." Lucy pushed a crayon drawing into her hands. It showed an explosion of colors that vaguely resembled a forest.

"It's beautiful," Nora said. "Did you eat already?"

"Dad made lasagna," she said. "It was delicious."

She looked toward Daniel, who was watching the exchange. His lips pressed into a thin line. "I know you like us to wait until you get home, but..."

"No," Nora said sharply, then softened. "It's okay, I under-stand. I had to stay to clean up... a mess."

"What kind of mess?" Lucy asked.

"It's not important." She shook her head.

"You want a glass of wine?" He gestured to the end of the counter where three bottles of wine sat on their side in a small wooden wine rack she had received from her father years earlier as a birthday gift.

She shook her head. "No, thanks. I'm fine."

"You don't look fine." He stepped toward the bottles of wine anyway. "A drink might help."

She moved toward him. "I'm not hungry either."

"Did you eat on the way home?"

"No, nothing like that," she said. The sharp, tangy smell of dead birds still lingered on her clothes, and it had killed her appetite.

"Don't be ridiculous. It's still warm." He gestured to the table. "Sit down, and I'll take care of everything."

Her head started to throb, and she nodded while dropping

into a seat at the table. "I'm not hungry... after what happened this morning."

"The garlic will help with that," Daniel said.

She surrendered. "Yes, alright, and I better have that glass of wine too."

"You won't regret it," Daniel said.

Lucy ran over with her backpack and jumped into the seat next to her. She pulled out an oversized book. "Mommy, I need help with my homework."

"Ask your dad." Nora pressed her eyes closed and rubbed her temples.

Lucy thrust the book into Nora's view. It was a book about birds.

"What makes you think I know anything about birds?" Nora nudged it away.

"Lucy," Daniel scolded while dishing up a slice of lasagna. "Give her some time to relax."

"But Mommy knows all about birds. She helped me put up the birdhouse in the backyard. Remember? I need to write a paper about them. I need to give a show-and-tell about my favorite bird. What's your favorite bird, Mommy?"

"I don't have one," she said.

"But I saw the feather in your room. And Dad said you had a whole flock of birds visit you today."

Nora gave Daniel a sharp look. "What?"

Daniel brought the food over to the table and placed it in front of her. "Oh, I didn't mean to suggest Mommy is an expert at birds," he said to Lucy. "She had a bad experience with them this morning. I was just trying to explain what happened in a way..."

"You found a feather?" Nora asked Lucy.

"On our sidewalk. I put it on my dresser."

Nora swallowed. "Why did you put it up there? Throw it in the garbage."

Lucy looked confused. "But I can use it for my show and tell."

"You're not going to use it for anything. Throw it away."

Lucy's expression was both stunned and hurt. Her eyes widened, and her bottom lip trembled. "I just... I just wanted to use it..."

Daniel gestured for her to leave the table. "Hey, that's enough," he said, placing a hand on Lucy's shoulder and nudging her away. "Now's not the best time."

Nora took a deep breath. After Lucy walked out of the room, she turned to Daniel and continued, "Why did you tell Lucy about the birds?"

"I let it slip, sorry, and she wanted to know," he said. "She deserves to know the truth about what happens sometimes in nature. I didn't give her all the gory details."

"I don't want her to have it."

"She's a kid, Nora," Daniel said in a low voice. "She went out to play in the snow for a few minutes after school. I didn't see the feather, or I would have thrown it out."

Nora nodded. "Please, just get rid of it."

"Sure." Daniel walked back to the kitchen, poured her a glass of wine, then carried it to the table a minute later.

Lucy's quiet sniffles came from somewhere just out of sight as Nora sipped her wine.

"Mommy," her daughter's voice came sweet and soft. "I'm sorry I made you mad."

"It's okay, sweetheart," Nora said. "I just had a really bad day at the parlor."

Daniel stepped over to Lucy and crouched beside her. "Let's see if we can find you a different show-and-tell project."

"I can't do birds?"

"Let's choose a different one this time. Okay?"

Lucy's shoulders drooped. "Okay," she said softly.

Daniel led her into the living room, where she grabbed

another book off the coffee table and flipped sluggishly through the pages.

Only a minute later, he came back and sat beside Nora, leaning closer and staring deeply into her eyes. "What's going on with you? You were talking in your sleep last night."

"I was?" she said. "What was I saying?"

"I couldn't understand—just mumbling. I think the stress is getting to you."

"To put it mildly."

Daniel was watching her, waiting for her to 'snap out of it.' She hated this part.

"I need some time." She avoided his gaze.

He nodded slowly. "I'm doing my best to hold things together, but I can only handle so much. I can't do all of this alone, and I sure as hell can't do it if you keep pushing me away."

"I'm not pushing you away." She raised her voice.

"I know things have been difficult lately for both of us, financially and in other ways. But you haven't been present for either of us. Are you having trouble with your father again? Is that what's going on?"

Nora's eyes teared up. She met his gaze. "It's not my father. Not this time."

Lucy came over and sat at the table between them with sad eyes as she flipped through the pages of a book on cats. Daniel sat down beside her and leaned in.

"You've got a lot of toys in your room," he said. "Maybe use one of the gemstones from the science center for your show-and-tell."

She shrugged and frowned.

The wine had started to kick in. Their conversation didn't seem as heavy anymore, and the tension seemed to melt away.

Something from across the room caught her attention—a faint rustling sound like paper fluttering in the wind. She turned her head toward the patio window. The sun had already gone down, but the blinds were still open, and the deep blue sky created an ominous backdrop to the trees and the house next door.

Something hovered just beyond the glass. An outline of someone staring back at her.

With a gasp, she pushed her eyes shut. When she opened them again, it was gone.

 ❦ 12 ❧

It was impossibly dark outside. Nora stood alone in the front room of the parlor, and there were candles flickering all around her—on shelves, on chairs, on the floor. How and why had Ally lit them all?

Where were the bustling pedestrians and the traffic?

The smell of blood caught her attention, and she glanced down. The glass, feathers, and carcasses were gone, except for the dark streaks of blood still smeared across the floor.

"Ally?" she cried out. Her sister had to be there somewhere, either in the back room or behind the front desk.

The front door clicked and then creaked open slowly. An icy wind swept in around her.

She gasped and stepped back, but her shoe slipped on the blood. Catching her balance, a shadowy figure emerged from the darkness outside, followed by a rustling sound like dried leaves scraping across the floor.

Not a figure—a swarm.

Blackbirds. Dozens of them. Their forms emerged from the shadows like ink bleeding through paper. Their ruffled feathers twitched in the dim light as they moved toward her, fluttering to life, staring at her with unblinking eyes. They came in and swarmed across the floor. One of them cawed and then the others, louder and louder, into a chorus that became deafening within seconds.

Stumbling backwards, she scrambled to hide. How had they gotten in? Who had opened the door? Had the window repair technician left it open? Had she? So many of them flooding across the floor. The birds seemed lost and confused. Had they come back to find their friends?

She fell back. The pain surged through her spine, and she struggled to stand, the blood smearing everywhere—across her clothes, hands, elbows.

Their focus turned to her. They moved toward her, their wings fluttering wildly, convulsing like the spasms of a death rattle. It was just like she'd seen the other birds do after crashing through the glass. One by one, they hopped closer, clicking their talons against the hardwood floor. The chaos grew louder until their squawks filled her ears.

"Ally!" she cried out again. "Dad!" she cried even louder.

Hadn't her sister gone home?

Hadn't *she* gone home? She remembered eating supper with Daniel and Lucy, but then nothing else.

Scrambling to stand, her feet brushed against their feathers, and her shoes came down on one of them who had ventured too close, its wings crunching beneath her feet. She looked toward the hallway for an escape. There was the back door into her father's apartment, although the hallway seemed to stretch out further than it should have. And there was the séance room and her office. She had no time to plan. She ran as fast as she could. The darkness seemed to swallow the light around her as their presence blocked out the lights.

She hurried into the séance room and slammed the door behind her.

"Please," she gasped, her voice barely audible over the chaos. "Someone help me!"

Backing away from the door, her heart pounded. She could

hear them coming up and pushing against the door. It squeaked and rattled with the weight of their shuddering bodies. Their beaks pecked and tapped against the door with relentless energy. Every part of the door cracked under the driving force, and she expected the thing to crash in at any moment.

She cried out, then clamped her hands over her mouth. Maybe if she stayed quiet, they would go away. What did they want from her? Had they come to remind her of what had happened that morning? She pressed her eyes closed and listened to her chest heaving with silent sobs. She was trapped. How could any of this be real?

The door splintered further. Their beaks broke through like jagged knives, slicing through the edges first, then along the bottom edge. They were creating a gap large enough to slip through. They came in one by one with eyes blazing with fury. Each flew around the room in a tornado of aggression as she pushed back against the shelves lined with the séance props. A few of the items crashed to the floor as she clawed at the wall behind her.

"Go away!" she screamed.

Running her fingers along the table behind her, she found the obsidian mirror and held it up with both hands, shielding her face. She prepared to do battle with them just as the weakened door cracked apart, and the blackbirds surged in.

They flooded the small room with feathers flying in every direction, brushing against her skin like icicles. They dodged around her feet, legs, chest, and up near her face, screeching into her ears and scratching. She slammed the mirror down against their bodies. The glass cracked against them, even as they continued to claw at her. One by one, she knocked them out of the air. Her screams died in the chaos.

One of them dropped in front of her eyes, digging its claws into her chest, staring back at her with dead black eyes. She ripped it away with both hands, dropping the mirror in the process and squeezed until it stopped moving.

Silence filled the air, and the birds dissolved like wisps of smoke. Within seconds, only the stench of blood still remained.

The door to the room was still wide open, and someone appeared in the doorway—the same tall, shadowy figure she'd seen earlier in the corner of the séance room and outside through her patio window. He was cloaked in shadow, his head hanging, tilted to the side. His eyes were wide yet... dark. Blackened pits that focused on her. She tried to back away further until her back hit the wall.

When the figure spoke, Nora's blood ran cold. She gasped for breath to scream, but nothing came out.

"Nora," he whispered in a low voice. She'd heard that same voice in her parlor not too long ago. A client? "You don't know what it's like to have your heart torn out." He stepped toward her and extended his bony hands toward her throat. "But you will."

She screamed.

"Nora!" Daniel's voice came from somewhere within her fog.

Her eyes snapped open, and his face came into focus. His eyes were full of fear and concern as he reached out to touch her hand cautiously.

"Nora, wake up," he said. "You're having a nightmare."

She forced her eyes to stay open. If she closed them again, the nightmarish figure would be standing there, waiting for her. The dark presence hovered in the space between them for a few seconds until it faded away.

"Gabriel," she said.

13

"Who's Gabriel?" Daniel asked first thing in the morning.
He'd asked the same question right after she'd
awakened from her nightmare, but the terrifying vision was too
fresh in her mind to talk about it then. And he hadn't argued.
He'd only comforted her for a long time, falling asleep with his
arms wrapped around her. It had taken her much longer to drift
back to sleep again—maybe hours. But now, Daniel needed and
deserved an answer.

They were both getting ready in the bathroom, standing side
by side in front of the mirror. He was combing his hair without
saying anything, but he glanced at her often with a concerned
look in his eyes. How would she explain what had happened with
Gabriel without reliving the nightmare from the previous night?
There was no way around it.

She applied less makeup than she would have for a normal
day at work. The eyeshadow that would have made her eyes
more piercing was absent, along with the darkened lipstick and
dark, fitted blouse, skirt, and polished leather boots that she
considered a costume. She left her silver ring on the counter,
along with her crystal earrings. She could pick all of that up later

after her visit with Gabriel. But she wanted to tone it down until after talking with him. She wasn't performing for anyone that morning. She was just Nora, and that made it so much harder to get ready.

"He was a client of mine," she said. There was a bit of jealousy in his eyes. "He stopped by the parlor a couple of weeks ago. No big deal."

"Someone special?" Daniel asked.

"No," Nora rolled her eyes. "Nothing like that, Daniel. He was just another client. I took his money and gave him a reading, and he..." The memories came back, but she struggled to answer. "Things went off the rails. He caught me lying. It was really humiliating. I did my best to calm him down, but you know how difficult it is to deal with someone when they're upset. After things fell apart, he ended up storming out of the parlor."

"What do you mean things fell apart?" Daniel asked.

"Some of the equipment malfunctioned. It's hard to explain unless you were there. Impossible to explain." She took a little more time touching up her lipstick, hoping he would drop the subject, but he wasn't looking away from her, so she continued. "I was just putting on my regular performance like I always do for everyone, and things went off the rails. He called me a liar."

"But you *were* lying, right?" Daniel asked.

She cringed and shook her head. "You don't understand."

Daniel smirked. "Help me understand."

"Ally was improvising with a little trick," she said. "It fell from the ceiling... onto Gabriel."

Daniel's eyes widened. "And that's when he blew up."

She nodded.

He cringed. "No wonder he was upset."

"It was just a little mistake," she said. "It's impossible to control everything in there. Ally works most of it from the back room now. We improvise. We do our best. I only get a few customers each day, so we do our best with what we have."

"Did you at least give him his money back?" Daniel asked.

"He never asked for a refund, but Dad made it clear he wouldn't get one anyway."

"Your dad was there?"

"He heard the shouting and came out."

Daniel cringed again. "Your dad…"

"He was trying to help."

Daniel opened his mouth as if he wanted to say something else but closed it again.

"It's okay though," she said. "I'm planning to stop at his house this morning to return his money. That reminds me, can you please take Lucy to school this morning? Since I woke up late?"

He nodded. "I can do that."

"Are you upset?"

He shook his head. "No."

She could see from his face he wasn't.

"How do you know where he lives?" he asked.

She continued getting ready without meeting his gaze. "I have his address from the form he filled out when he signed up for the reading, and I plan to give him a full refund and apologize."

He shook his head again. "Not a good idea. It's better for you to let it go. You might make it worse."

"You should have seen the pain in his eyes—pain that I caused him. He was devastated. I think he was the first customer who ever saw me for who I really am—the fraud that I am. I was ashamed of the way he looked at me. I know I made a mistake by not doing more to calm him down and doing the right thing. But I saw the way he looked at me—through me. I thought he might jump over the table and…"

"So now you're having nightmares about him?"

She nodded. "I have to go back and at least return his money."

"Someone should go with you."

"I can handle it myself. Please don't try to stop me."

"What about Ally? Can't she go with you?"

"She has to open the shop and get it ready. I have a client scheduled this morning as soon as I get there. I promise this won't take long."

"Why do you want to risk starting another fire? I agree that you didn't handle it well, but... you shouldn't go back there or even try to contact him. I'm sure you feel bad about what happened, but maybe this is a life lesson. If he was as angry as you said... it's not safe to go there alone."

"It happened two weeks ago," she said again. "I'm sure he's calmed down by now."

Daniel pushed his lips together and turned back to brushing his hair. His eyes hardened a bit. "Maybe it's time we talked about finding you a new career."

"Doing what, Daniel? We've already had this conversation. I'm not changing careers. The solution is simple: I'm going back to Gabriel's house to refund his money, and I'm going to apologize. This thing is haunting me."

He nodded slowly without looking over. "I can see that. Maybe I can take the day off work to go with you."

She shook her head. "You can't afford to miss another day of work."

He seemed to consider it for a moment then surrendered. "At least text me the address, just in case."

"It's not too far from here. Everything will be fine."

"Call me as soon as you get there, at least so I know you're safe."

She took a step toward him and touched his arm. "I love how you're always trying to protect me."

"Someone has to."

She stared at herself in the mirror, letting her hair fall loose over her shoulders. The woman staring back at her was nothing like the smooth character she portrayed at the parlor as Madame Lenora. This woman's face was full of fear and regret, and without the makeup, she looked vulnerable. It was better to meet Gabriel like this—without her mask—better to show him her true emotions. But was that even possible anymore?

✵   14   ✵

Nora parked her car on the street in front of Gabriel's house. It was in a residential area of the city, crowded with historic Victorian-era homes that the upper class must have flaunted and cherished at one time, except most of them now looked run down and neglected. Gabriel's porch was sagging to one side, with the wood siding desperately needing a fresh coat of paint. This was not the home of a rich patron seeking a thrilling encounter with a dead loved one, but someone who had truly spent his last dollar to meet with her out of desperation, and the thought stabbed at her heart. She had made the right decision to return the money.

The engine ticked softly as her gaze followed the sidewalk leading up to his front door. There was nothing to prevent her from completing her mission. No excuses.

Wrapping her coat a little tighter around her chest, she hesitated with one hand on the door handle. Visions of how he might react ran through her mind. Would he fly into a rage again or graciously accept the refund and her apology? Either way, it was clear she *had* to go through with it.

Her recent nightmare was still fresh in her mind—the birds crashing into the parlor, her frantic escape to the séance room, and Gabriel's menacing presence as he reached for her throat. Despite everything, she needed answers and closure as much as he did, if only to stop the relentless guilt that gnawed at her conscience. It was now or never.

Stepping out of the car, the sound of someone walking nearby caught her attention. An old man in a hooded parka from the house next door was picking up his mail. He kept his gaze down with a cautious demeanor as she stepped up onto the sidewalk and trudged toward Gabriel's front porch.

After reaching the door, she paused. There were no signs that anyone was even home. The blinds on the front windows were shut, and the windows were dark.

Would she need to come back later?

God, I hope not. It had taken all her courage to stand there now.

She took a deep breath and pressed the doorbell, hearing the faint sound echo from behind the door. Only silence.

Pressing the doorbell again after a long moment, someone's voice broke the tension.

She turned around to face the old man she'd seen at the mailbox. His face looked familiar.

He was walking toward her, cutting across the lawn. "You're wasting your time."

Nora spoke politely. "Why is that?"

"He's gone."

Nora's heart sank. She *would* need to come back.

After he moved into her line of sight, she recognized him.

Father de la Cruz.

He seemed to recognize her at the same time. "Nora?"

"Father Tony?" she said. "I didn't know you... lived there."

"I do." He smiled warmly.

Nora glanced across the yard toward the old man's house. "This is... unexpected."

"Likewise," he said. "Are you looking for Gabriel?"

"Isn't he home?" She gripped the envelope tighter and

searched the porch for a place where she might place it for Gabriel to find later.

"Do you have some mail for him?" the father asked. "Are you dropping something off?"

"I have a letter," Nora said.

Father Tony kept approaching, shaking his head. "I'm afraid he'll never get it." He squinted at her. "Were you... a friend of his?"

She hesitated, then forced a smile. "An old friend. I haven't seen him in years." The lie hurt. She had come there to show her authenticity, and she had failed within minutes of arriving. Her father's words echoed through her mind.

You were born to hustle.

"You're a little late." The father sighed and motioned for her to step down from the porch. He glanced at the envelope and then looked into her eyes. "He was a nice enough guy. Shame what happened."

Nora's chest tightened. "What happened?"

He gave a solemn look. "Didn't you hear? Mr. Flores passed away. Suicide. You didn't hear?"

"No." Nora took in a quick breath. "I didn't know that."

He gave her a sympathetic look. "Sorry to be the one to tell you. I guess he didn't know what else to do. Ran out of money after his wife died last summer in a car accident, and he let his career fall apart. I was the last one to talk to him. He said he'd spent every penny he had trying to fix things, whatever that meant."

The words hit Nora like a punch to the gut. She had also come to fix things.

Father Tony gestured to the door. "I'm helping his brother take care of the place until he can get up here to clear out the place. His brother lives in Los Angeles, but the two didn't get along, so I'm sure he'll wait until the weather warms up."

"I see."

The father glanced at the envelope in her hand. "Would you like me to give that to his brother?"

She stared down at it, then held it out. "Yes... please."

He accepted it with only a casual glance before slipping it into his pocket. "I'll see that his brother gets it."

"Thank you." A sense of relief washed over her after surrendering the cash. At least she'd done the right thing for once.

"Is your contact information inside the envelope?" he said. "In case his brother has questions?" The old man shivered in the icy breeze.

She hadn't written anything on the envelope and had left just a short note inside. She had planned to apologize in person. "Father Tony, it's not—"

"Here. Let's step inside, get out of the cold, so we can talk." He moved toward the door, opened it, and led her inside before Nora could object. After closing the door behind them, he pulled the hood off his head.

Brushing back a tuft of his thinning gray hair, he flipped on a few lights on his way toward the kitchen. The air was uncomfortably quiet and not much warmer than outside, but at least they were out of the wind. A stench hung in the air—something rotting?—but it also smelled of burnt wood and animal dander.

Walking toward the kitchen, she paused at the framed photos on the walls. One face stood out immediately. Gabriel. Maybe now he could rest in peace. Another face caught her attention. A little girl with Gabriel's distinctive green eyes. It could only be Anna, the girl Nora had pretended to contact in her séance, and she couldn't help but feel heartbroken for Gabriel and their tragic lives.

Father Tony stopped and followed her gaze. "Did you know his daughter?"

"Not really."

"She was a lot like her father, in many ways. She inherited his love for animals. But after Mrs. Flores died, I didn't see either of them around much. He didn't get along well with his siblings, according to his brother, but I take it all with a grain of salt. Everyone has their baggage. Love, loss, regret—emotions always cloud opinions, whether we like it or not."

Nora couldn't look away from Anna's photo, staring into the girl's eyes with a heavy heart as if to truly connect with her spirit.

"Sweet kid," Father Tony said. "Died of leukemia just a few months ago after a long battle, you know... or maybe you don't know."

Nora couldn't look away from the photo, her vision blurring as her eyes started to water. The pain welled up in her chest.

"He tried everything to save that girl," Father Tony continued. "And I mean *everything*. Experimental drugs, holistic medicines, treatments in other countries. He refinanced his house, but the medical bills kept piling up. All of his efforts failed, and when she passed away, Gabriel fell apart."

When Nora looked up, she caught Father Tony staring toward the back door. She followed his gaze but saw nothing. "Something wrong?"

He seemed to snap out of it. "No," he said. "Sorry. I was just remembering something. That's where he died. I'm the one who found him."

Nora took a sudden breath and met his gaze.

He continued, "He was one of my parishioners for years—a devout Catholic, until his wife died. Then he fell away from the church, and I only ran into him once in a while, despite being neighbors. We'd both go to the mailbox at the same time, just after the mail truck came through, and sometimes he'd have something to say—sometimes we'd have a laugh—but most of the time it was a simple hello and then we'd retreat to our houses. He was an odd character—very strange—as I'm sure you know. He became even more introverted after Anna died. The only time I ever saw him was when he'd walk out to the mailbox every morning, so after he didn't show up for a few days, I knocked on the door, found it empty, and invited myself in.

After I found his cat digging through the garbage outside, I knew something wasn't right. I searched the whole house before I found him dead near the back door."

He looked at her, furrowing his brow. "You okay?"

Her vision swayed a bit. "Yes, it's just a lot to take in."

"Your face is a little pale."

"Is it?"

"You want to sit down?"

She shook her head and glanced across the living room. A massive fireplace filled an entire wall, constructed with irregular stones that didn't quite match the decor of its surroundings.

Something like white fibers was sprinkled over the couch and recliner, and several animal cages of varying sizes were stacked against a far corner. "He had pets?"

Father Tony swallowed, followed her gaze, and then frowned. "He had a lot of pets... at one time. That was his profession before things fell apart—a veterinarian. But you probably already know that."

"Yes," Nora said softly. He'd caught her in a lie but hadn't seemed to notice.

"He wasn't the same after Anna died, let me be clear. After the man lost his family and then his livelihood, things spiraled quickly, from what I could tell." Father Tony glanced around the area and then stared solemnly into Nora's eyes. "That kind of tragedy changes a man. It eats a hole in his soul to where I figure he lost touch with reality near the end, which led to his suicide. Gabriel always believed in the afterlife, but after Anna died... he dove headfirst into everything connected with the occult. He became obsessed with finding a psychic in the area who might help him contact Anna in the afterlife. He was hellbent on exploring every avenue to contact his daughter, including some very *extreme* measures."

"What do you mean by extreme?"

"I won't go into too many details because thinking about it makes me ill, but when I first came in here to look for him after

I hadn't seen him for a few days, I found some mighty awful things lying around the house. Dead things. He took..." Father Tony's voice cracked. "He took some of the rescues with him."

Father Tony stared into the distance, then winced and shook his head. "There's no sense in ruining your appetite. I'll stop there, but he was a sick man... in the end."

Nora's imagination ran wild, filling in the gaps in the father's story, and she hoped her conclusions weren't true. She remembered how Gabriel had come into her parlor seeking help, his unkempt appearance and desperate stare, and she'd run him through the mill like everyone else.

"He only wanted to talk with his daughter," Nora said.

Father Tony met her gaze and nodded. "That's right." Stepping toward the end table near the couch, he picked up a letter. "I found this near his body when he died. A letter he wrote to Anna after she died. He poured his heart out in it, talking about his love for Anna, how he wished he could have fixed her like he could fix animals. Said he hoped the next life was kinder to him." He handed Nora the letter. "But he wrote something on the other side, probably right before he killed himself. He was in a dark place in his last moments."

Nora's hands trembled as she accepted the letter.

Father Tony continued, "His letter to Anna is on one side. On the other..."

She opened the letter, unfolded the paper, and scanned the words. Gabriel's handwritten text to Anna was raw, filled with love and sorrow. His grief poured off the page, and each word stabbed at her heart.

My sweet Anna,

I've prayed until my throat is raw, but my cries go unanswered. My life is a hollow shell without you. If there is a door between this world and then next, then I'll find it and bring you back to me. I won't stop until I hold you again in my arms.

Forgive me, my sweet angel, for what I'm about to do.

Love always,
Dad

"I didn't know," she whispered to herself.

He gave her a sharp look. "Didn't know what?"

She shook her head quickly and put on a smile. "I... I just didn't know he was suffering so much."

The old man softened. "Yeah. Well, he wasn't one to bother anyone with his troubles. He used to care for the strays in the neighborhood... with Anna's help, and he occasionally took home a rescue. But that... changed after she died."

"How did that change?" Nora asked.

Father Tony flipped over his hand while gesturing to the letter.

Nora turned it over and read the other side. The handwriting was sloppier, heavier with sharp angles and incomplete sentences. The tone was much darker and full of hate.

"It's pretty much a suicide note," Father Tony said.

She gasped in a breath at the first words:

Liars. liars. every damn one of you. sick. fake. animals. you gave me hope then ripped it away. i only wanted to see my ANNA. my sweet girl. to hear her laugh. see her smile. the only light i ever had. i'll find her. whatever it costs. Moloch will bring me to her. HE alone. shows the way.

mediums. psychics. palm readers. FRAUDS. you'll feel it. all of it. the pain. the fire that eats through me. i'll make you feel it. i'll watch the flames rip through your souls. burn you in hell. no mercy. no forgiveness.

there IS a hell. demons wait there. waiting for you. they'll drag you down. screaming. i'll dance in the light of it. see you soon

She stood breathless after reading it then glanced up to meet his gaze. He stared back sympathetically.

"Yeah, I've never read a suicide note before," he said. "But I'm sure this ranks up there with the most twisted."

Nora handed the letter back to him. She couldn't push it away fast enough. "I don't know what to say."

"Exactly." Father Tony slipped the letter into the envelope and dropped it back on the end table. "I had the same reaction. Like I said, Gabriel was in a dark space in his final days."

Gabriel's icy words reverberated through her whole body. It shook her to the core of her soul. It was clear he'd branded her as one of the *frauds*. Maybe not *just* her, but the note read like his final judgment on her failures as a medium. She pushed the thoughts away and continued, "What did you mean when you said Gabriel took some of the rescues with him?"

He stared at her for a long moment before answering. "Being a veterinarian, he knew how to put animals to sleep..."

"I see," Nora said.

"I found his three dogs in there, the ones he'd adopted over the years." He gestured toward the fireplace against the wall. "He burned them in there. It's hard to believe. Stacked them in there like cordwood. Not much left of their bodies by the time I found them, but I could see there was a symbol branded into their sides. An occult symbol, like he'd tried to do devil worship on them or something. He'd burned the same symbol into his own chest. I saw it clearly. He was shirtless when I found him lying on the floor."

Nora swallowed hard, trying to process the disturbing images flooding her mind.

Father Tony gestured out the window toward his house. "Another one of his animals must have escaped before Gabriel got to him, although he didn't escape getting branded. I have him at my house. A white cat named Blanco. It's old and a bit... opinionated, which is why I guess nobody else stepped in to adopt him after the tragedy. Nobody wants to adopt an old cat, especially one with an occult symbol on it. He was Anna's cat. Another stray Gabriel rescued from the street. I've been feeding him since Gabriel died, but pets are expensive. Do you have any pets?"

Nora shook her head. "We've talked about it."

"Blanco is a good cat, but I already had three before this happened. Blanco is just one too many for an old single man." He watched her expression. "I'm worried I might be forced to take him to the shelter."

Silence passed between them as guilt washed over her. The rage in Gabriel's note stung in a way she'd never experienced before. She might not have caused his suicide, but she sure as hell had enabled it. "I'll take him." The words were out before she could stop them.

The father looked surprised but also relieved. "Thank you," the man said with sincerity. "You won't regret it."

She nodded as a sinking feeling filled her chest. How was she going to feed another mouth? And this would open another rift between her and Daniel, although Lucy would no doubt jump for joy.

"Let's stop by my place then. I'll give you whatever you need to care for Blanco. He's gotten all his shots, neutered, and all that stuff. Like I said, he's a good cat. He just needs a little patience, that's all. And a loving owner."

"Thank you," she said.

Father Tony hesitated. "Maybe you should meet him first before you commit to taking him home?"

"It's not necessary. I'll stop back after work today and pick him up on my way home."

The father nodded. "Blanco will be waiting."

❧ 15 ❧

Ally tensed when her father walked into the front office. It wasn't usual for him to come up there, especially not that early in the morning. He was carrying a bottle of glass cleaner and a rag, heading toward the front window without saying anything. She let him trudge up to the glass alone. It was awkward enough just having that silence between them—especially after the way he had berated her and Nora the previous day, after the birds had crashed through the window.

He glanced back, but she looked down. The last thing she needed was another confrontation. When she looked up again, he was using the glass cleaner to wipe a section of glass near the door.

"Father Tony's guys did a good job," he said, without glancing back at her.

"We're lucky he stopped by." Ally paused in her work. It was difficult to focus anyway. She set her pen down and waited for the inevitable argument.

Her father shook his head. "No, he probably just wants you to join his church or something. That's why he stopped by. The broken window was just an excuse. It got his foot in the door."

"You don't know that, Dad."

"That's how they are, Alison. Religious types always have a hidden agenda."

"Not everything's a conspiracy theory."

"I know what I'm talking about." He wiped another section of the glass, then stepped back. "Just stay away from all of them. Don't let them indoctrinate you."

Ally folded her arms over her chest. "What are you so afraid of, Dad?"

He turned around and faced her for the first time. "I'm not afraid of anything."

"Sure sounds like you are."

His face hardened a bit and then softened. "I only want the best for you and Nora."

"Really? Is that why you fuss so much about my going to school? You're afraid I'll learn something about the world? Maybe I'll learn you were wrong about everything."

He gave a little grin. "Your mom had the same attitude. Stubborn as hell. You look an awful lot like her now. In that light... that expression. That's the way she used to look at me when we argued, when I nudged her in the right direction."

"You mean when you convinced her to drop out of college."

"Claire dropped out on her own," he said. "Nobody forced her to do anything."

"That's not what she told me," Ally said.

"Oh? What did she tell you? Did she tell you about all the nuts she was hanging around with in college? I bet she left that part out. They were messing with her mind, but I steered her away from all of that. I saved her."

A real hero. Ally opened her mouth to say it, but then she shut it again. It was better to let it go.

Her dad continued, "That's how they ruin your life—they get you to think they're smarter than the rest of everyone, smarter than the rest of the world. Pump up your ego. Fill your mind with lies and call it truth. They did a number on Claire before I stepped in to straighten her out."

"You straightened her out, all right, Dad." She spoke before she could stop herself and instantly regretted it.

His eyes narrowed—she'd gotten to him.

Instead of retreating, she continued. "You're just afraid someone in your family will be smarter than you."

His grin widened a bit. "Your mom never had that much of an attitude. Not like you."

Ally braced herself for more. She could feel the tension rising between them. This was how it always started—just casual talk at first, and then *wham*—he would launch a curveball aimed at her heart. He would masquerade an insult as a compliment. She waited for the words that would stab her heart, and she dreaded it.

Picking up her pen again, she stabbed at the paper. "I'm tired of all the patronizing talk, Dad. I don't need any advice from you. About college. Maybe I'll do something different from what you want me to do. Maybe I'll go in a different direction. Or maybe I'll stay here after all. It's *my* decision."

"Your future is here." He gestured toward the front window. "Study all the books you want—but keep in mind, *this* is your home. You've got to make a living somewhere, so it might as well be here. Learning about devil worship, ancient curses, and magic won't pay the bills. It means nothing unless you can make money from it. Be practical."

She rolled her eyes—she couldn't help it. "There's more to life than money."

"That's true," he said, "but not much more. I won't give you any more advice today, but I hate to see you waste your time on worthless college classes. You're just like your mother in a lot of ways, but she eventually woke up."

The years of bitterness were welling up. Ally struggled to hold it back. "If you hated Mom taking college classes so much, why did you marry her?"

He glanced down and then took a step toward the back of

the parlor. "I didn't hate anything about her. She made me laugh. And she was smart."

"Smarter than you," Ally said.

He clenched his teeth and then nodded. "Probably. I know you're just trying to get under my skin—but you're right. She *was* smarter than I was. And I'm glad she was smart enough to drop out of college when she had the chance. It was the best decision of her life. She needed to get away from all that weirdo-demon crap. That's where it started—the books. If you read too much, pretty soon you think you've got all the answers. You stop listening. You stop seeing reality for what it is. You lose touch with reality and start making mistakes. She made plenty of mistakes, but I steered her away from the worst of it." He met her gaze and paused. "I just don't want you to make the same mistakes she did."

His expression softened, and the tension faded a bit. He rarely talked about their mother's college years. This was an opportunity to catch a glimpse into their family's past. "What mistakes?"

"Too many books," he said softly. "They had her stepping out on a tree limb. Seeing how far she could go before it snapped."

Ally scoffed. "Mom never did anything reckless like that."

"She did, and she's a lot like you." He glanced at her and held her gaze. "That's what scares me."

Ally studied his face, waiting for it to harden again. "That's interesting. This is the first time you've admitted you're scared of something."

"Oh, there are plenty of things I fear," he mumbled. "I've seen enough to know not to venture too far from home. Trust your old man on this. It's my job, you know—to steer you away from fatal mistakes."

"I'm not stupid."

"I never said you were."

"You sure act like it."

He took another step toward the back and shook his head. "You think I don't know what I'm talking about, but I do."

"Getting a college degree wasn't a fatal mistake, Dad."

"You don't get it," he said. "It's not the degree—it's the... direction—the path. I'm trying to steer you away from—"

"From what?"

His face hardened a bit. "You've got to just trust me on this. Be careful of what you put into your mind. People will try to plant a lot of seeds there. You won't notice it at first, but they'll grow and grow until you don't notice them anymore. They'll become part of you. Some of them aren't so bad, but some of them will eat away at who you are. Stick to the basics, Allison. It's better that way."

"You mean I should forget everything I learned in college?"

He let out an exasperated sigh. "No, I'm not saying that."

"Ignorance is not bliss."

"No, I'm not saying that either. Just... keep your eyes on what's real. There are too many distractions out there."

The door cracked open, breaking their fragile conversation. Nora stepped inside a moment later. She glanced at their father and then looked away while closing the door behind her.

Their father stepped out of the way when she came in. He lifted the glass cleaner and rag a little higher as if to justify his presence, but he stayed silent.

After removing her jacket, Nora moved into the parlor while staring at the front window. "It looks like new."

"They did a good job." He turned away from them. "Just keep your eyes on your purse with those guys. They offer their help now, but nothing's free. Payment comes later, when they pass around the collection plate."

After mumbling a few more things under his breath, he scanned the glass for a long moment and then headed back to his apartment.

Nora and Ally stood silent until he was gone. After his door clicked shut, Ally let out a breath and stepped out from behind the front desk.

Nora gave a little laugh. "What was that all about? He came out to check on you?"

"Probably." Ally rolled her eyes. "You know how he gets."

Nora nodded with a little smile. "I know."

But there was something *off* in her sister's expression. A distant stare Ally had seen before when something was bothering her.

"Is everything all right?" Ally asked.

Nora didn't answer right away. Instead, she stepped behind the counter and glanced at the floor. When she looked up again, anguish spread across her face. "I stopped by to see Father Tony this morning."

Ally stared into her sister's eyes. "Why?"

"I learned a few things... about Gabriel. He left a suicide note." Nora dug into her pocket and took out her phone. "I have a picture of it here."

She brought the photo up on her phone's screen and showed it to Ally. There was a handwritten note, scrawled almost illegibly.

Ally scanned each word carefully with wide eyes. Heartache rippled through her chest. "Oh, my God. That's horrible."

"He's talking about me, Ally," Nora said. "The frauds, the fakes in his note. That's me."

"You don't know that."

"I do. Father Tony said Gabriel sought help from other psychics in the area, but I was the last one. I'm the one who pushed him over the edge. Me. I'm the one in the note—the one that... failed him."

Ally stepped forward and embraced her sister, slipping her arm around Nora's shoulder and propping her up gently. "You didn't know. We certainly would have done things differently."

"I'm not sure how I can deal with this." Nora backed away

and crossed her arms over her chest. Her gaze dropped to the floor. "It's heartbreaking."

Ally nodded. "Yes, but... there's nothing we can do now. He made that choice, not you."

Nora shook her head slowly. "It won't be easy to focus today."

A moment later, the bell above the door rang. A middle-aged woman stepped inside, wearing a long overcoat. She glanced around the front entrance and shut the door behind her as the cold air rushed in around them.

"I'm wondering if you can help me," she said in a small voice. "I'd like to speak with my deceased husband. Jacob."

Ally straightened behind the counter, and her sister did the same. Skimming through the names on the schedule for that day, Ally forced herself to concentrate on the task at hand. Still, it wasn't easy to set aside what she'd just seen on Nora's phone. Gabriel's suicide note still reverberated through her mind. "Do you have an appointment?"

The woman smiled politely and shook her head. "Do I need one?"

"It's not necessary." Nora's posture and expression completely shifted a moment later. The distress on her face melted away. She was slipping back into her Madame Lenora persona. She stepped out from behind the front counter and extended her hand toward the woman. "My name is Madame Lenora. What's yours?"

❧ 16 ☙

Nora arrived home late that evening and set Blanco's animal carrier down in the living room, along with a bag of cat supplies Father Tony had provided to get her started. Daniel and Lucy watched with wide eyes as she opened the gate door. Blanco stepped out cautiously, and Lucy's delighted squeal filled the air. The cat's snowy white fur was like a massive snowball against their dark floor. He sniffed at the air, then stepped toward the couch where Lucy sat cross-legged. Her crayons were scattered across the coffee table beside a stack of coloring books.

"Mom!" Lucy's face lit up, and she jumped toward the cat, extending her hands with a wide grin. Blanco froze and moved back, staring at Lucy with wide, curious copper eyes.

"Lucy, don't scare him," Nora said. "Let him come to you."

Lucy didn't seem to notice. Instead, she dropped onto the floor in front of Blanco, moving down to his level to face him head-on while whispering into his face, "Hi, Blanco, you're so pretty."

Despite Lucy's excitement, the cat moved closer to her, and its tail flickered lazily. Within moments, he was pressing his head against her outstretched fingers. Lucy's giggles filled the room.

Nora and Daniel exchanged a glance, although she could see he wasn't entirely convinced by their new houseguest.

"So this is the cat you mentioned, Blanco?" There was skepticism in his eyes.

"Are you mad?" she asked.

"Not mad, just concerned."

Lucy scooped the cat into her arms, and he settled into her embrace as if he had already made himself at home. Twisting him around to play, her gaze stopped on the scarred symbol Gabriel had branded into his flesh. "What's that?"

This is what Father Tony had talked about—the abuse. Nora had seen the scars when she'd picked up Blanco at the father's house after work. A series of lines and some smaller circles stood out against his pink flesh. The cat must have gone through hell.

"He was... mistreated," Nora said.

Daniel moved in to have a look and frowned. "Oh, my God. Poor guy."

Lucy turned him back upright as if to hide what she'd discovered and then squeezed him tighter. "It's okay, Blanco. You're safe here with me."

Nora turned to Daniel. "I know what you're thinking."

He folded his arms across his chest. "What am I thinking?"

"How are we going to afford a pet along with everything else in life?"

He tilted his head. "That thought did pass through my mind."

Nora paused before answering. Telling Daniel she'd adopted Blanco to mend some of the bad she'd caused wouldn't cut it—not without a long explanation. It was easier to justify it in a more practical way. "I just couldn't leave him," she said. "The owner was going to take him to the rescue, and you know what happens to a lot of animals there if nobody adopts them."

"I do."

Nora dug through the bag of cat supplies that Father Tony had given her. Just the essentials, but it helped. Cat food, a litter box and litter, water bowls, a brush, and... a small bronze medal tied to a red knotted cord. It looked like an old coin, except that a large cross dominated one side. Each quadrant of the cross bore a different letter: C S P B. And more letters ran around the edge of the coin: V R S N S M V - S M Q L I V B.

A gift from the priest to bless Blanco's new home?

Placing the medal on the counter, along with everything else, she turned back to Daniel. "So, we can keep him?"

Lucy glanced back with wide eyes. "Dad, we can't get rid of him. He's perfect."

"We *did* talk about getting a pet someday," Nora said.

"Are you sure about this?" Daniel asked her. "We didn't really talk about it until now."

Nora considered her response carefully before answering. "Put him on probation? We'll give him a few days and see how it goes." Her gaze lingered on Daniel. She searched his face for signs of a compromise.

He sighed. "Fine. But you're cleaning the litter box, Lucy."

Lucy grinned and squeezed Blanco tighter against her chest. "I love him."

Nora stepped toward Daniel. "Thank you," she whispered.

Only an hour later, Nora settled into her side of the bed and picked up her favorite book from the end table. For the first time that day, she felt at peace with herself and the world. Blanco was in Lucy's room, and Daniel had shown no signs of stress over their new pet.

She wanted to express how she felt about the cat. Bringing him home in the animal carrier had reminded her of the day they'd brought Lucy home after giving birth, carrying her inside the house in a car seat on that cold afternoon. It almost felt like they had adopted another child, in a way. And Lucy now had a baby brother, in a sense—at least someone to play with and learn responsibilities. She kept silent, though, not wanting to spoil the peace between them. She had even considered falling asleep early that night until Lucy rushed into the bedroom, her face full of tears.

Nora sat up. "What's wrong?"

Lucy crumpled over Nora's legs and cried, wiping her tears on the comforter. "Please don't kick him out. He made a mistake."

"Who made a mistake, honey?"

Lucy continued crying until Daniel got out of bed and went to the doorway. Lucy followed him. "Don't kick him out, Daddy," she said.

"What did he do?" Daniel hurried out into the hallway with Lucy following behind. Their footsteps clomped down the stairs, and only a few moments later, Daniel's exasperated voice echoed through the air. "Nora?"

Something had happened. Dread swept through her body as she stood and headed downstairs. She found him standing in the kitchen. Judging by the cringy expression on his face, something was very wrong. He was staring at the floor, focused on something hidden behind the island between them. A familiar smell caught her attention—the faint metallic scent of blood.

"Daniel?" she asked.

"Over here," he repeated with a strained voice.

Circling the island, she followed his gaze down to a headless blackbird. Its feathers were ruffled and bloody, and there were bits of feathers and blood streaked across the floor leading out toward the back door. It was the same type of bird that had crashed through the parlor glass. Her stomach churned, and she turned away in disgust. "What happened?"

Daniel gestured toward the patio. "Blanco must have gotten out."

"I didn't mean to," Lucy said suddenly. "He was scratching at the door."

"Nobody blames you," Daniel said to her. He turned to Nora.

"Lucy let him out, I suppose, and Blanco decided to bring home a present for us."

Nora looked toward the patio door where Blanco sat grooming himself as if nothing had happened. His fur was ruffled now, with bits of blood and feathers stuck in it. "Where's... the rest of it?"

"I suppose he left that outside," Daniel said.

Lucy stared at the bird, inching forward, until Nora pulled her back. "Don't touch it."

"I wasn't—" Lucy cried. "Blanco brought it inside, but he didn't mean to scare us."

The cat looked over at them with an almost smug expression, his tail twitching as if proud of what he'd done.

"I'm sure he didn't." Nora pulled Lucy into her arms. "Go wash your hands now."

"I didn't touch the bird." Lucy tugged at Nora's pajamas.

"It doesn't matter. Go wash your hands anyway."

"Please don't get rid of him," Lucy begged. "He didn't do anything wrong."

"We'll talk about it later," she said, pushing Lucy toward the bathroom.

"Is he in trouble?"

"Go wash your hands," Nora repeated a little louder, and Lucy started trudging toward the bathroom with her face down.

Nora stepped over beside Daniel and calculated how best to clean up such a gruesome mess.

"Are you sure you want this?" Daniel asked softly while leaning against the kitchen counter.

Nora glanced back to make sure Lucy was out of earshot. "It's just a cat," she said. "I'm sure he won't cost *that* much."

"Especially on a bird diet."

Nora studied his face for a moment and decided he was being sarcastic. "That's what they do—they hunt. It's normal."

"I know," he said. "It's just... gross. Aren't you worried this sort of stuff might traumatize Lucy?"

"We'll just need to make sure she doesn't let him out again. There's a learning curve, you know." Nora glanced toward Blanco. She could think only of Gabriel's tragedy. Blanco was her responsibility now, her penitence for what she'd done, and she was determined to go through with it. "He's an old cat. He won't be around much longer."

"That's not reassuring," Daniel said. "He'll die right after Lucy warms up to him. She's too young for that kind of trauma in her life."

"Did you see the look on her face? She loves him."

"We should have talked about this a little more before bringing him in."

"I didn't have time."

"We said we'd think about it for a few days, right?"

"We have to keep him," she said finally. "We're keeping him."

Daniel looked at her and didn't look away for a long moment. "Alright," he said, "but you know I don't like surprises. No more pets for a while. Agreed?"

She nodded once. "Agreed."

Blanco meowed softly. Nora couldn't shake the feeling that the cat knew exactly what he was doing.

❧ 17 ☙

Nora awoke to something crashing against the floor. Had something dropped from a shelf? Or something had fallen over downstairs? Had she dreamed it? Peering through half-open eyes, she listened to the silence for as long as she could until her eyelids fell shut again. Nothing she couldn't deal with in the morning.

But then it came again. Something crashed downstairs in the living room. An intruder? Her eyes snapped open wide, and she turned to face the door.

Daniel sat up at the same time and switched on the lamp. "What was that?"

Before she could answer, Lucy screamed. "Mom!"

Both of them jumped out of bed. Nora's heart pounded. She raced out into the hall first, switching on the lights, and nearly tripping over some of Lucy's toys in the process.

"Mom!" Lucy cried out again from her bedroom.

Nora burst into Lucy's room and embraced her daughter. She was trembling and pointing frantically toward her closet. "There was a man. He was standing right there."

Daniel came in a moment later. "What's wrong?"

"She saw something in her closet."

He stared into the open doorway for a moment, then hurried over and flipped on the closet light. Pushing aside her clothes and some toys along the bottom, he looked around the room then dropped to the floor and checked under the bed. "Nothing."

"I saw him," Lucy said. "He was watching me."

Gabriel's face flashed through Nora's mind. "Are you sure it was a he?"

Lucy frowned. "Don't you believe me?"

"Yes," Nora said. "We believe you. What did he look like?"

"It was dark," she said.

"Oh, honey." Nora pulled her in closer and brushed the hair out of her face. "Are you sure you didn't have a nightmare?"

"I was awake, Mommy," she said. "He woke me up."

Daniel spoke in a steady voice. "Can you describe him for us?"

Lucy turned her face away from the closet. "I didn't see him very well."

"You just said you saw a man." Daniel frowned.

"I saw his eyes," she said. "He had wide black eyes... like circles. Wait." Lucy jumped across her room and came back with her iPad. After waking up the screen, she turned it toward them. "I took a picture."

The grainy picture showed a shadowy form, blurred and indistinct, but undeniably there. The eyes were round, just like Lucy said, but a little sharper and set back within the darkness.

A chill swept down Nora's spine.

"That's... interesting." Daniel stared at the image.

"I told you so," Lucy said.

"It's okay, sweetie," Nora said to Lucy. "You're safe now."

But she could feel *something*. A presence that hadn't been there the day before. Nora glanced around Lucy's room. "Where's Blanco? Did he come in here?"

"Yes," Lucy said.

Nora relaxed a bit and gave a little smile. "Maybe you just saw Blanco watching you, playing a trick on you from the closet."

Lucy shook her head. "It wasn't Blanco. A man. His eyes were up there." She pointed toward the top of her shirts in the closet.

"Cats can jump very high," Nora said. "He could have easily climbed up there."

Lucy stayed quiet and shook her head, but Nora wasn't going to argue with her daughter.

Daniel stared into the closet. "There's no one in there."

Lucy burst into tears, pushing her face into Nora's chest. "I'm not lying," Lucy said. "I saw him."

Nora tightened her embrace. "We believe you."

"We're not saying you lied," Daniel said. "Something happened, and I'm guessing Blanco had something to do with it."

"No, Daddy. It was a man, as tall as you," Lucy said. "And he wanted to hurt me."

"Nobody wants to hurt you, sweetheart," Nora said.

"This man did."

Nora exchanged a long look with Daniel until he turned away and walked out into the hallway. He stood there, silent and still, scanning the area before heading down the stairs.

Nora turned back to Lucy. "Come on, sweetheart, let's get you back to bed."

"Can I sleep with you?" Lucy pleaded.

Before Nora could answer, Daniel came rushing back up the stairs and stopped in the doorway. His eyes were wide and he gasped a breath.

"Did you see him, Daddy?" Lucy asked. "Is he there?"

Daniel gave a small, nervous shake of his head. "Call the police."

~

TWO POLICE OFFICERS ARRIVED TWENTY MINUTES LATER AND searched the house methodically, sweeping their flashlights over the mess and into the shadows. They went through every room, even going down into the basement and peering up into the attic. Nora stayed in the kitchen with Lucy, while Daniel followed them around, explaining what had happened.

Someone had ransacked their home, knocking books and potted plants off the shelves, and framed pictures off the walls. A bookcase lay on its side beside a sofa cushion that had somehow landed across the room. Soil from the plants and shards of glass littered the floor.

Blanco was sitting on the counter, watching them all with an amused expression.

"There's no sign of forced entry," one officer said while jotting notes in a small pad.

"No," Daniel confirmed.

The taller of the two officers shifted his attention to Nora. "Ma'am, has there been any tension in the house lately? Arguments, maybe?"

Nora's face flushed warm. "Excuse me?"

"Sometimes in cases like this, it turns out to be—"

"We didn't have a fight, if that's what you're suggesting."

"Just covering all the bases." The officer held up his hand.

They walked around the area near the patio door and stopped. One of them squatted down and focused the flashlight on the floor beside it.

"Did anyone hurt themselves lately?"

The blackbird.

Nora caught her breath. "The cat," she said. "We adopted a cat yesterday, actually, and he dragged in a headless bird last night. I cleaned up the blood, I thought, but I guess I missed some spots."

"You have a pet." The officer nodded as if he understood. "I was going to bring that up next as a possibility."

He opened the back door and used his flashlight to illuminate every part of the backyard. A cool breeze swept in until he closed it again and turned back to them. He locked it and gave it a tug.

"I don't see any signs of an intruder," the officer said. "Do any friends, family, or neighbors have extra keys to the house?"

Daniel shook his head. "Nobody else."

Blanco strolled in at that moment, prancing over near the officer and sitting at his feet, watching them from beside the back door as if he expected them to let him outside. The officer glanced down with a hint of a smile.

"I'm going to suggest putting the cat in someone's room tonight with the door shut, just to see if that clears up any issues from happening again," the officer said.

Nora nodded. "I understand."

"Kids sometimes have quite an imagination," the officer said.

"It was a man," Lucy said from Nora's side.

"You've got a beautiful cat." The officer leaned forward and spoke down to Lucy. "Do you know that its eyes can reflect even the smallest amount of light? That's how it sees in the dark. You'll get used to having him around... in time."

Lucy didn't respond.

The officers put away their flashlights and headed toward the front door. "I think everything here is... wrapped up then. Let us know if you—"

"I took his picture," Lucy said. She hurried away to her bedroom and came back holding up her iPad. "See?"

The officer leaned down to look and then nodded. "A trick of light. This is exactly what I thought. You can see how the light from the tablet is reflecting off the cat's eyes." He gave Lucy a sympathetic smile.

"It's not Blanco," Lucy said softly.

Nora pulled Lucy closer. There was something odd about the picture, the way the shadowy form reminded her of what she'd seen in the séance room the previous day. Maybe they were all imagining things. Maybe Nora's career had somehow spilled over into the darkened imagination of her daughter. A flash of guilt swept through her.

"Ma'am?" the officer said. "Please try to get a good night's sleep."

Daniel walked them to the door. "Thank you, Officer. Sorry for dragging you over here in the middle of the night."

"No problem at all," the other officer said.

When they were gone, the house fell still again. Daniel started cleaning up the mess, while Nora took Lucy back to bed. When she returned to him, the frustration on Daniel's face was clear.

"I'm not sure a pet is the best thing for us right now," he said.

She didn't respond. Instead, she took over where Daniel left off and swept up the shards of glass from the broken picture frame that seemed to have scattered under everything. Blanco sat on the windowsill now, watching everything with wide copper eyes.

You know what's happening, don't you?

Did you do this on purpose? I brought you home to make peace with Gabriel.

Lucy's voice broke the silence. "Mommy, you saw it too, didn't you?"

Nora turned toward the stairs. Lucy was standing at the top, her face heavy with sadness. "Go back to bed, sweetheart."

"But—"

"Now," Nora said a little firmer.

Lucy hesitated, then her shoulders slumped as she shuffled toward her room.

Daniel finished placing the books and plants where they belonged, although he'd missed some of the soil and glass under the furniture. "I'll clean up the rest tomorrow," he said. "Is there anything else I should know?"

The question caught her off guard. "What do you mean?"

"The guy who owned this cat..." he said. "What was he like? This isn't normal."

She looked at him but kept her feelings guarded. "I know it's not normal. Nothing in my life is normal right now. I just felt bad they were going to take it to the shelter."

Daniel stared at Blanco for a long moment, then walked away with his head down.

Nora followed him upstairs a short time later, turning off the lights on her way toward their bedroom. She carried Blanco into the laundry room down the hallway, where they had also put the litter box, and closed the door.

Blanco let out a soft rumbling purr that sounded a bit like laughter.

$\maltese$ 18 $\maltese$

Nora started her morning coffee with her mind in a haze. Daniel had finished getting his decaffeinated blend, and he drank it with his hands curled tightly around the mug while standing across from her.

"You didn't sleep much." He met her gaze.

Nora smiled. "Neither did you."

With a shrug, he looked away. "Too much on my mind."

"We can handle one cat," she said.

He nodded. "I'm more concerned about her imagination."

"She's just being a kid," she said. "She didn't see anything last night."

Daniel nodded. "Good. I know. She went right back to sleep. She was a little freaked out this morning. I had to get her clothes from the closet because she wouldn't go in there."

"That's how kids are," Nora said. "Kids have nightmares. We just need to keep Blanco out of her room for a while." Nora pictured the cat's intense stare and that smug grin. "I'm sure you had some nightmares when you were a kid."

Daniel kept silent and stared out the window for a long moment. "My nightmares were a little different," he said quietly.

"Mine had a face and a name. I used to lie awake at night, waiting for my dad to come home from the bar."

Nora closed her mouth. He had hinted at this story a few times during their marriage but had never filled in the details, and she had never asked.

"He used to come in the front door and slam it shut. But then I'd hear him come up the stairs." Daniel let out a humorless laugh. "I'd count the steps after he reached the top of the stairs. I knew exactly how many it took to get to my room. If he stopped at twelve, then I knew I'd be okay. But if he got to thirteen…"

Nora reached out and touched his hand but kept quiet.

Daniel continued, "It didn't happen all the time, only when he'd had a bad day at work. But it would take Mom a while to calm him down. Then he'd take it out on her. I promised myself I'd never ever let my kid feel that way. Last night when Lucy looked at me, when I saw her face… What was I supposed to do?"

"You did everything right," Nora said. "That's the most important thing."

"Maybe for now," he said, "but what if it continues?"

A flurry of footsteps burst into the kitchen. Lucy's face was full of fear. "Mommy! Daddy! I can't find Blanco!"

Nora's heart skipped a beat as she feared another disaster coming. Her coffee was ready, but she left it behind to hurry upstairs toward Lucy's bedroom. "He's probably hiding somewhere."

"Did you let him out again this morning?" Daniel called out from behind them.

"I only let him out last night," Lucy said quietly.

"Then how could he have gotten out of the laundry room?" Nora asked.

Lucy stopped in her bedroom and sat on her bed with her face down. "I lied," she said quietly. "I let him sleep in my room. He looked so sad in there. I couldn't leave him alone like that."

Daniel stepped into the doorway a moment later. "He'll be fine alone. You can't let him out like that anymore, okay? Especially after what happened last night."

"But he looked so lonely in there," Lucy said. "And I was scared."

Nora sat beside her daughter and pulled her closer. "We need to keep him safe at night so he doesn't try to run away. He probably misses his previous owner, but he's our responsibility now. We have to take very good care of him. Do you understand?"

Lucy nodded.

"It's going to take a while for him to feel comfortable living here with us," Nora continued. "He'll be just fine sleeping in the laundry room for now. Okay?"

"Okay." Lucy nodded and glanced around her room. "But where did he go, Mommy? I'm scared something happened to him."

"Nothing happened to him." Daniel turned around to leave. "I'll go look around."

Nora also stood up. "We should all look for him."

They split up. Nora and Lucy searched the bedrooms side by side while Daniel circled through the living room and kitchen, dropping to his knees a few times to check under the furniture.

"Blanco!" Lucy called out every few seconds. "Where are you hiding? Please come out."

"Lucy," Daniel said, "you didn't let him outside again, did you?"

She shook her head. "I'm afraid he'll hurt another bird."

A noise came from Lucy's room. Nora followed it, stopped at her daughter's closet, and opened the door.

Blanco was there. He was sitting perfectly still in the back corner, his white fur standing out like a ghost against the darkness, and his wide copper eyes seemed to turn black now. Not black. Hollow.

Nora blinked, and they were copper again. The shadows had played tricks on her. She shuddered and stared at him for a long moment. Shaking away the image, she finally called out, "Found him."

Lucy let out a delighted squeal, and within seconds both she and Daniel stepped into the room. Lucy dropped to her knees in front of the closet and climbed inside.

"What are you doing in here, Blanco, you silly cat?" Lucy asked.

"I thought you already looked in here," Nora said.

"I did," Lucy replied. "He wasn't in here before."

"He must have run in here after we left the room," Daniel said.

"Wouldn't we have seen him?" Nora asked.

He shrugged. "He's a cat."

Lucy inched toward him, but Blanco still didn't move. "Come here, Blanco. We looked everywhere for you. Where did you go?"

Daniel leaned down to get a better view. "He'll come out on his own. Don't scare him."

Nora snapped her fingers behind Lucy to get the cat's attention. "Come on, Blanco."

Lucy inched a little closer.

Blanco let out a low growl and retreated further into the closet.

Lucy pulled her arms away and glanced back. "Something's wrong with him, Mommy."

"Let him come to you, honey. Don't force him. He's just not used to us yet."

Daniel came up beside them, extending his hand toward Blanco while rubbing his thumb and index finger. "We're not going to hurt you, little guy."

Blanco growled again until Lucy started making whistling noises. His eyes widened—almost too wide—as if he'd seen something they couldn't. When she stopped, he moved cautiously toward her and then jumped forward into her arms.

Lucy scooped him up and carried him out of the closet while

stroking his fur. "Don't do that to me again, Blanco. You scared us."

Blanco let out a loud purring sound, but there was a strange look in his eyes, and the corners of his mouth were turned up at the edges just a bit, like he was in on a joke that no one else knew. The cat met Nora's gaze with a piercing stare, and it caught her off guard. His unblinking eyes seemed to sink back into his head, leaving a blackened pit in their place. A moment later, they returned to normal. This time, she stumbled back, catching herself on Daniel's arm.

He helped steady her while watching her with a curious smile. "You okay?"

Nora hesitated to answer and avoided Blanco's gaze. Had she really watched the cat's eyes change color? Not just the color. Their *depth*. It had to be an illusion. Some sort of play of light when he turned his head to the right angle. Finally, she nodded. "Sure."

"You'll be alright," Daniel said to Nora. Then he left the room.

"Of course you will," Lucy said into Blanco's face. "You'll be *just fine*."

"Put him in the laundry room now, honey. You need to get to school."

"Can't we take him with us?"

Nora shook her head. "Not today. No. Hurry, or you'll be late."

Lucy pretended not to hear, instead she lifted Blanco into the air and made kissing noises. "Isn't he *beautiful?*"

"Yes," Nora said. "Put him in the laundry room *now*."

Leaving the bedroom together, Daniel was already rushing out the door. He would be late, and the tension showed on his face. It was better to let him go without saying goodbye.

On their way to the laundry room, Lucy stopped and turned her face up, offering her best pitiful expression. "*Please* let me take him to school with us, Mommy. He'll be so lonely in there without me. He might even cry."

"He won't cry." Nora raised her voice. "We don't have time for this."

"Mommy, please, can I take him with us?" There were tears forming in her eyes. "He's shaking. He knows I'm leaving, and he's scared. You can't leave him home alone, Mommy. Can't we take him with us just this once?"

Nora hesitated. If she allowed Lucy to take him this time, she would keep asking again and again. But it was difficult to say no. They had the carrier. He could stay in there and then she would drop him off at the house on her way to the parlor. It wasn't *that* far out of her way.

"Fine," she said. "Just this once, but he stays in the carrier."

❧ 19 ☙

Nora headed out into the traffic toward Lucy's school and immediately regretted her decision to take Blanco home again before going to work. It wasn't a huge hassle, but the traffic was worse than usual. Catching a glimpse of Lucy in the rearview mirror, Nora watched her daughter in the back seat, bundled in her favorite pink coat with one arm stretched out around Blanco's carrier, strapped into the seat beside her as if trying to comfort him. Lucy was leaning in toward him, and her lips were moving silently near his face as if holding a private conversation.

The morning frost hadn't yet melted along the edges of the windshield, and Nora turned the heater up a notch. A chill passed under her jacket. The vents were blowing the air across her face, yet it wasn't warming up. It always took time for the heater to kick in, but something wasn't right. Placing her hands over the vent openings, she adjusted their direction a bit, yet the air seemed to flow around her no matter where she aimed them.

Nora glanced into the rearview mirror at Lucy. "Did you crack the window open back there?"

"No, Mommy."

She pressed the window controls up anyway, to make sure all of them were shut tight, but another chill swept through the air.

Is something broken?

Glancing back at Lucy again, her daughter was peering down between the bars of Blanco's carrier, poking her fingers inside and brushing his fur with her small fingers.

"Don't tease him," Nora said.

"I'm not."

"Maybe keep your fingers out of his carrier too."

Lucy gave a small laugh at the suggestion. "He won't bite me."

"I know, but I'm sure he doesn't like getting poked like that."

Lucy pulled her fingers out.

Snaking through the traffic, the stoplights seemed to conspire against her, hitting every one of them. The school wasn't too far ahead—she could see the white property fence in the distance—but the morning traffic was always a bit tricky to navigate along that stretch of road. Too many parents dropped their kids off at the same time, and the morning commuters always struggled impatiently to get around them.

The icy air lingered even after a couple of minutes.

What the hell?

She put her hands over the vent openings again. The air was still cold, and it felt even colder over the passenger seat.

Glancing again at Lucy in the mirror, she asked, "Are you cold back there?"

"No, Mommy."

This isn't right.

Pressing her lips together, she dismissed another chill creeping up her spine. Then Lucy spoke in a low voice not her own.

"I'm going to burn in hell for your sins, Mommy."

A surreal silence fell between them as Lucy's words hung in the air. Nora took a long moment to process what her daughter had said.

The words stuck in Nora's mind. Had her sweet eight-year-old actually said that?

It didn't make any sense.

Had Nora imagined it? Or misunderstood? Sometimes Lucy did that, mispronouncing a word so poorly that it sounded like a curse word. Only after putting it into context would Nora realize what Lucy had intended to say. Sometimes, bitch meant beach, fuck meant fork, shit meant sit or sheet, and then she'd laugh to herself. It happened occasionally. Or, it used to happen when Lucy was much younger.

But this... Lucy hadn't slurred her speech or garbled any words. She'd said it as clearly and casually as if mentioning she planned to read a book when she got home.

Nora stared back at her daughter's face in the rearview mirror. The look on Lucy's face hadn't changed.

I misunderstood her.

It was the only possibility. Any other answer was... crazy?

Or maybe she had said that to the cat? But what a strange thing to say, even to a cat.

The thought that Lucy had intentionally said that to *her* seemed... impossible.

Nora gripped the steering wheel a little tighter and fought to stay focused on the traffic. She needed to make a right turn soon, but Lucy's words ate at her mind.

"What?" Nora asked finally.

Lucy looked up, staring curiously from the backseat. "What, Mommy?"

"What did you say?"

Lucy looked confused and hesitated to answer. "I don't know."

Nora turned her attention back to the road. No, she couldn't have heard it correctly. By the look on her daughter's face, she had said something similar, but not *that*.

A few seconds later, Lucy's voice rose again above the car's rumble. "Daddy too. I'll go first so you can watch me burn." Lucy's voice was lower this time, with a dark tone.

Nora turned down the car's heater fan to listen—it wasn't making a difference anyway. "What are you saying to Blanco?"

"Nothing."

"Why did you say it like that?" Nora looked at her in the rearview mirror. "Are you pretending?"

"I didn't say anything." Lucy gave a nervous smile.

Nora hadn't actually watched her daughter say it. Her daughter's expression was a picture of innocent confusion, and her little eyes widened even more as Nora continued to study her. "Are you playing a game with me?"

"No."

"You said something about Daddy. It's okay. It just... sounded different."

Lucy frowned. "I didn't, Mommy."

She *had* heard Lucy's voice, hadn't she? She wasn't imagining it. It was as clear as anything she was saying now. Lucy had a vivid imagination, so maybe her daughter had blurted out something without any thought. But still...

Her heart beat faster. She gripped the steering wheel a little tighter, speeding to make it to the next light, although she failed to make it in time before it turned red. Beating her palm against the steering wheel, she took a deep breath and closed her eyes for a moment.

Had she taken on too much that morning by agreeing to bring Blanco along? She hadn't wanted to disappoint Lucy, not after the frightening event the previous night. Was Lucy just doing what any child would do in the back seat with a cat— holding an imaginary conversation?

No, not her imagination. Not Lucy playing a game. It was real.

The voice came again. "I'll scream until your heart shatters."

This time, Nora had caught Lucy's lips moving in the mirror. She'd watched Lucy saying the words. Her daughter had said them intentionally, staring *straight back* at her with an intensity completely unlike Lucy. The words were sharp and low, as if she were pretending to be somebody else. Someone with an especially cruel demeanor. She had become someone unrecognizable.

"Lucy," Nora cried. "Why are you… What are you doing?"

Lucy stared wide-eyed in the mirror back at her. Her daughter had returned. "What was I doing?"

"What are you doing with your voice?"

"I'm not," Lucy said with a fearful expression as she shrank back against the seat. "Mommy, you're scaring me."

Nora squeezed the steering wheel, her gaze jumping from the traffic around her to the rearview mirror. The school was just ahead, but she couldn't shake the sense that either she was losing her mind or Lucy had seen something on TV that she shouldn't have. "Lucy, please tell me. What did you just say?"

"I don't know." Lucy's voice was desperate and tears welled up in her eyes. "I didn't say anything, Mommy."

Glancing back at Blanco, his face pressed against the bars with a piercing gaze aimed directly at her.

"Mommy?" Lucy asked in a trembling voice. "What's wrong?"

Nora twisted around in her seat to face Blanco directly, if only to get a better look at the cat's expression in that moment, the way he seemed to mock her. A scream filled her mind.

Not a scream. A car horn.

The jarring sound of a car horn shook her nerves, and she almost lost control of the car. Looking ahead, red brake lights filled her vision. She couldn't stop in time. Jerking the steering wheel sharply to the right, she had a split second to act, swerving onto the shoulder and slamming on her brakes. The force threw them to the side, and Lucy shrieked as they came to a stop.

She had narrowly missed hitting the car in front of her.

How fast had she been going?

Too fast.

Her heart raced as car horns blared past her. One driver even shouted curses from his open window, although his words were thankfully muffled behind the glass. With her pulse thumping in her ears, she took a minute to grasp the gravity of the situation.

"I'm sorry," Nora whispered, looking at her daughter's face again in the rearview mirror. "Are you okay back there?"

Lucy nodded, but she had draped herself over Blanco's carrier. "Yes, Mommy."

The cold air was gone, and the heater blew warm air again. She switched it down, and took in a deep breath before pulling out into traffic again, joining the line of cars leading into the school's parking lot. With trembling hands, she focused on her breathing to clear her mind.

What the hell had just happened? Lucy's 'pretend' voice had thrown her off and Blanco... The way he had stared at her, like he was in on the joke. The whole thing unnerved her like nothing she'd experienced before.

Lucy was sniffling, her tear-streaked face turned to the window, and Nora wanted to jump out and wipe those tears away.

"I'm sorry," Nora said again in a lighter tone. "I was distracted. You said something... Please don't cry."

"I'm sorry," Lucy said in a sweet soft voice. The ordeal had taken a toll on her. Another frightening event she didn't deserve.

Dropping off Lucy in front of the school, Nora gave her daughter a heartfelt "I love you." Lucy still had tears in her eyes when she got out of the car and turned back to wave goodbye to Blanco. It was heart-wrenching to watch Lucy leave like that. What would her teacher think when she stepped into class with a trail of dried tears down her cheeks?

Bad parents.

Nora's heart sank. She had scared Lucy and still had no explanation for the strange voice. Blanco was watching her from the backseat and she met his gaze. He had that look again—cruel amusement.

Didn't all cats have that expression?

But she could almost hear him laughing in her mind, wild laughter at how she had almost gotten them all killed.

Before leaving the school drop-off zone, she threw her door open and jumped out of her car.

One of the teachers standing nearby called out to her, "Everything alright?"

No, definitely not alright.

She didn't answer. Instead, she went into the back seat, unbuckled Blanco's carrier, and spun it around so it faced away from her before buckling it up again.

She held a smug grin as she drove away.

Nora stepped into the parlor, and the bell above the door chimed. Pushing her way inside, she bumped Blanco's carrier against the door frame. He made no sound. The icy wind swept in around them until she pushed the door shut.

Ally glanced up from behind the front desk, sliding a stack of papers into a folder. She smiled at Nora before her gaze dropped to the carrier. Her face lit up.

"Oh my god, you got a cat!" Ally said, hurrying around the front desk to meet them. She dropped to her knees and peered through the carrier door. "Wait, Nora, you adopted a cat?"

"It's complicated," Nora said. She put the carrier on the floor, where Ally peered inside with a wide grin. Nora turned away after Ally started making kissing noises and speaking in baby talk as if Blanco might understand anything she had to say. When she turned back, Ally was unlatching the door.

"Don't," Nora said sharply, holding out her hand.

Ally hesitated, her fingers pausing on the latch with a confused expression. "Why not?"

Nora glanced at the carrier's door. Blanco was staring back at her with an incessant grin. He wasn't shifting around inside the carrier, trying to get out, like a normal cat would do. His wide eyes were locked onto her.

"He's fine in there," she said.

"Okay..." Ally slowly backed away. "What's his name?"

"Blanco," Nora said.

"Blanco," Ally repeated. "The white cat. Gato blanco. He looks Persian. Am I right?"

"I'm not sure." Nora kept her gaze on the front desk and the papers in the folder Ally had gathered for her. "Who's our next client?"

"I'm sure he's Persian," Ally said, standing up while staring down at the carrier. "He's beautiful."

"Do you think so?" Nora opened the folder.

"Is he going to spend the day with us?"

"I'm not sure yet." Nora let out a slow breath and tried to focus on the papers in front of her. Ally had prepared everything, organizing all the detailed client notes into an easy-to-read outline.

Client's name: Lizzie Raymond
Seeking: Closure with deceased husband, Michael Raymond
Recent loss, wealthy, skeptical

The notes almost filled an entire page. Nora skimmed over them but had to read them a few times to absorb them. Her mind kept jumping back to Lucy's voice in the car, how she'd spoken in that warped, unnatural way.

"Nora?" Ally asked.

She flinched and met her sister's gaze. "I'm sorry, what?"

Ally looked a little concerned. "What's going on with you?"

"Nothing," Nora said. "Just tired."

Ally gestured toward the carrier. "So if he's going to spend the day with us, what are we going to do with him? Should I put him in your office?"

Nora cringed. The thought of putting Blanco in her office

sent a chill up her spine. She didn't spend a lot of time in there, using it mostly for just breaks between clients and filling out paperwork, but the thought of Blanco staring at her again, like he had from the backseat of her car...

I'll go first so you can watch me burn.

Lucy *had* said that, hadn't she? Her daughter's lips had moved, and she had heard someone's voice—someone *else's* voice—coming through her daughter. But that was impossible, wasn't it? It was crazy—batshit crazy. Despite everything she professed as a "real" psychic, had the superstitions and nonsense finally caught up with her? Was even she starting to believe the lies now?

"Not yet," Nora said. "I think I should take him back home over lunch."

"Will he be okay in the carrier that long? You'll need to let him out at some point. He'll need to use the bathroom. You *did* bring a litter box or something, right? And water?"

Nora hadn't considered that, not in her rush to get to the parlor on time. "I... I didn't think this through."

Ally laughed. "Obviously. He could be a mascot, you know. White cats are seen in the spirit world as bringing good fortune, transformation, and as a sort of messenger from beyond. With those beautiful copper eyes..." Ally flitted her eyelids at him. "He looks mysterious enough. I think he could fit in well here. Clients would love him, I'm sure. We could make a place for him in the corner and put his litter box in the bathroom..."

"No." Nora shook her head. "I'll take him home... as soon as I can."

"Or you might ask Dad to watch him," Ally suggested lightly.

Nora cringed. "Because that'll go well. Dad would sooner throw him out onto the street than agree to babysit him."

"Okay, you're right. Not Dad." Ally glanced down the hallway toward the back. "There's not much space for him in his apartment anyway."

The idea of leaving Blanco in a position where he could

watch Nora didn't sit well with her, especially when she was trying to focus on her job, but there wasn't much room in their small parlor. Her office would have to do for now.

"In my office then," Nora said, "but keep the door shut."

Ally gave her a strange look, then lifted the carrier and walked Blanco back to her office. Blanco let out his first noise since they'd arrived, a deep throaty purr.

Only a short time later, the shop's door jingled again. Their first client of the day had stepped in, and Nora greeted the woman as she stepped into the front room—a middle-aged blonde woman with tired eyes and a nervous smile. She hesitated near the door, clutching the strap of her purse as if debating whether or not to turn back.

Nora stepped forward, slipping into her usual theatrics. "You must be Lizzie."

"Yes," the woman said with a shiver as she removed her violet scarf and jacket. She met Nora's gaze. "Madame Lenora?"

Nora nodded and shook the woman's hand with a gentle squeeze. "Pleasure to meet you."

Lizzie's fingers were cold, and she glanced around the shop before inching forward. "This is... quaint."

"Historic." Ally walked in and took her place behind the front counter. "The Vale family business has occupied this space for over seventy years. Three generations of psychics have given readings here."

The woman's face brightened a little and her shoulders relaxed. "Then I guess I came to the right place."

"You won't be disappointed," Ally said.

Lizzie let out a shaky breath. "I've never done anything like this."

"I understand," Nora said. "We'll take great care of you. Right this way." She gestured toward the back of the parlor.

They walked down the short hallway, turned into the séance room, and Ally closed the door behind them. The heavy velvet curtains draping the walls helped to muffle the sounds of the outside world.

Nora ceremoniously lit a candle at the center of the séance table, and Lizzie took a seat on the opposite side, watching Nora with wide eyes. This was the same process she went through with every client, but her hands trembled a bit more than usual, the events of that morning still echoing through her mind. The flickering flames helped to soothe her thoughts, so she lit a few more on a nearby shelf and shifted them a little as if that might help her contact the dead.

"How can I help you?" Nora asked while lighting some sage. She already knew the answer to that question after reading Ally's notes on the front desk but asked anyway. With a little puff, she blew out the sage and let the smoke rise from the embers as she placed it on a nearby shelf.

Digging into her purse, Lizzie produced a small photo of a middle-aged man and clutched it for a moment before placing it on the table. "My husband," the woman said, "he died a few years ago, and I'd like to talk with him again."

"Of course." Nora nodded, sat down in her seat, and held out her hands. The woman took them as the light from the flames danced around the room. "Let's both take a deep breath to help clear the space of toxic energy."

They both took a deep breath.

"Picture him in your mind," Nora said.

Lizzie nodded.

"I'm going to contact him," Nora continued, "and ask him to come forward."

Almost on cue, the air grew a little colder, and the lights flickered. Ally was doing her job perfectly, but the candle's flame on the table seemed to bend under an invisible strain as if someone were trying to blow it out. Lizzie was watching the flames with a fixed stare.

Was Ally pumping in too much cold air?

"We'll begin by closing our eyes now." Nora closed her eyes

halfway but kept them open wide enough to make sure everything was progressing as planned. "His name is Michael," Nora said as if she were just receiving the information now.

Lizzie flinched at the sound of his name. "Yes, that's my husband."

"Michael," Nora repeated. The candles flickered wildly again. "Please join us in this space. Lizzie is here and wishes to communicate with you. Please step into this space and make yourself known."

An icy chill filled the room.

Too much, too fast, Ally.

Nora held back a shiver as the temperature dropped even more. The candle's flame on the table between them still held that strange shape, creased to the side as if held down by an unseen force. Had Ally installed a new method to move the air around the room? The unexpected events weren't *bad*—they added a bit of mystery to the séance, if anything—but Ally should have warned her beforehand about the changes.

"I can see a spirit," Nora said. "Michael, please give us a sign."

An icy breeze—more like a wind—swept over them, and every candle in the room went out at the same time. Lizzie let out a startled gasp. This wasn't something they had planned. Nora swallowed a cry in her throat as the darkness and silence surrounded them.

Come on, Ally. Easy on the air.

"I can feel his presence," Nora said, forcing herself to speak in a calm tone.

Those were the cue words.

I can feel his presence. The words were intended to cue Ally to begin the next stage of the performance. Instead, a series of clicks and a thump came from somewhere behind the wall. Ally was no doubt working the switches, but judging by the silence, something had gone wrong.

"Yes, I can feel his presence," Nora repeated a little louder.

A moment later, the table rumbled to life, shifting and rising.

This was part of Ally's theatrics, but something was different this time. The spirit's glow wasn't there. According to the script, a spirit in the form of a soft glow should have appeared hovering above them—a wispy illusion generated using the same forgotten technology of Victorian Spiritualist mediums. Simple but effective. But instead, only darkness filled the room until the candle on the table burst to life again. It ignited twice as strong as before, burning with a strange green hue that lit Lizzie's face like a glowing emerald. Her eyes were wide and full of fear as she glanced around the room.

"Is he here?" Lizzie asked in a shaky voice.

"Please keep your eyes closed," Nora said.

The woman closed them again and squeezed Nora's fingers tighter as they held hands. "Is he alright?"

"He's at peace," Nora said. "He wants you to know he is surrounded by loved ones and is saying you don't need to worry."

The woman burst into tears. "I always worry too much."

The candle's flame wavered and then burst even brighter, as if someone had thrown accelerant on it. The intensity was magnified by the darkness around them, burning through the wick and the wax at an alarming rate. Despite the radiant surge, the chill in the air lingered. Squinting her eyes to block out the lime glow, she continued, "Is there a question you wish to ask him?"

"Yes," Lizzie said in a broken voice. "Yes, I want to ask him if he approves of my relationship with Charles Barlow. I need to get his approval to marry him. I won't go through with it if he objects."

The candle's flames puffed out a shiver of dark smoke. It twisted upward, writhing in the air before smoky tendrils broke off and branched out in every direction like fingers.

Nora stiffened. There was something strange about the way the smoke spiraled and churned without dispersing. Instead, it seemed to coalesce into a claw hovering above the candle's flame

—bony fingers grasping the silent air. The wisps of smoke drifted outward as if searching for their next victim. A chill ran up her spine.

Lizzie shifted uncomfortably in her chair but kept her eyes shut, even as the smoky forms moved toward her. A new tendril uncoiled like a serpent in front of her face. If Lizzie had opened her eyes at that moment, even a little, she would have screamed.

The forms moved with purpose toward Lizzie, brushing against the woman's cheek and across her hair, then slithered down the side of her neck, curling gently, almost tenderly, around her throat. Her eyelids fluttered, and she flinched, but that was all. How could she not feel the form touching her skin?

Nora wanted to jump forward and brush the smoke away from her client before it progressed any further, but doing so might break her out of the performance. If she could just hold it together for at least a few more minutes...

Her stomach churned as the smoke turned toward her and coiled around her own neck. She could feel it—an invisible pressure tightening like an icy rope around her throat. She swallowed hard but forced herself to stay composed. The candle's flame burned brighter, churning out more smoke.

She needed to put it out. Snuff it out. This was getting out of control.

Leaning carefully forward, she blew across the flames softly.

Nothing.

The flames didn't even flicker.

Another hard breath with the same result—the flame was unwavering as if they didn't exist in the same universe.

Her heart pounded.

The same thing was happening to Lizzie. Wisps of smoke thickened around the woman's throat, solidifying into something sinister. It was acting on both of them at the same time.

Nora slipped one of her hands away from Lizzie and swept it through the smoke, attempting to rip it away from the woman's neck. There was nothing to grab, nothing to fight, except the freezing air biting at her skin until it burned.

Panic rose in her chest. The pressure around her throat intensified, the thick smoke squeezing at her neck like a noose, and she couldn't breathe. She choked in a little air as her eyes widened. The smoke tendrils closed in and the world seemed to blur at the edges.

She gasped in a strangled sliver of air—

A scream tore from Nora's throat, and she pushed back from the table, nearly knocking over the candle on the shelves behind her.

Lizzie screamed a moment later, but the fear on the woman's face wasn't from what she'd felt moving across her neck. It was because of *her*. Because Nora had screamed.

"What happened?" Lizzie cried.

Nora couldn't answer right away. The candle's flame burned at its normal size again. Just a simple flickering flame. No icy tendrils around her neck. No surging flame. All of the smoke was gone. She caught her breath. "I... lost the connection."

"Why?" the woman asked. Her eyes were wide, her face full of distress. "Is something wrong?"

Nora shook her head and tried to throw herself back into the performance. "I'm sorry. Nothing's wrong. Sometimes I see... distractions."

"About Michael? Didn't he approve of the marriage?"

"He approves." Nora nodded. "He accepts Charles."

The woman's expression didn't change. Nora shifted back toward the table, reaching out to the woman's hands again, but she resisted. "Are you sure?"

Nora nodded again and again. "It's okay. You didn't hear his voice, but... it's okay."

She stared around the room like a child hiding from the boogeyman. "Is he... still here?"

Nora's heart still pounded in her chest as she took a deep breath to calm herself down. She needed to keep her client calm, but how could she do that if her own hands trembled? Still, she forced herself to engage with Lizzie. "I can still feel his presence. Do you have any other questions?"

The woman shook her head as she jumped to her feet and backed away. "I don't think I can continue with this," she said. "I'm sorry, but thank you."

Before Nora could reply, the woman stood and rushed out of the room. A minute later, the door's bell chimed with the door slamming shut behind her.

Ally burst into the room a moment later and switched on the lights. "Nora!" She reached for the candle on the table and snuffed it out with her fingers. "Nora, what the hell just happened in here?"

Nora was still trembling. Her heart beat a little closer to normal now, but her gaze stopped on the smoldering single candle at the center of the table. What else might have happened if she'd stared at it long enough? She touched her neck. "I'm not sure. Someone was choking me."

Ally paused and studied her for a moment. "Okay," she said in a calm tone. "We need to take a break."

Nora nodded, then stood up and gripped the edge of the table as though she might collapse at any moment. "I'm not... I'm not sure what I'm doing anymore. Ally, something went wrong, very wrong. Did you see what happened in here?"

"I saw everything through the mirror," she said.

"The smoke. There was something... *alive* in it." Nora swallowed and slumped forward. "This might sound crazy, but I think we might have conjured a real spirit or something. I keep hearing and seeing things. I almost crashed the car this morning because of Lucy."

Ally's eyes widened. "What happened to Lucy?"

"Nothing happened to her, but I heard her speaking in someone else's voice. And Lucy didn't even realize she'd done it."

Ally took her time answering. "Whose voice?"

"I'm not absolutely sure, but... it sure as hell wasn't *hers*. Do you remember a client from a while back, when everything fell apart? He caught us cheating and stormed out. A guy named Gabriel?"

Ally seemed to search her memory for a moment, then formed a knowing expression and nodded. "I do."

"He killed himself shortly after leaving here. I think it was him, but... speaking through Lucy, he said something like..." Nora forced herself to repeat the line as a wave of emotion swept through her. "... 'I'm going to burn in hell for your sins, Mommy.' Is that insane or what?"

Ally stared at her curiously. "It's not insane. Of course, it's possible, but how do you know he killed himself?"

"I went to his house, to make amends, and his neighbor told me. That's where I found Blanco. He was Gabriel's cat."

Ally's eyes widened. "So *that's* where you got him."

"I only went there to bring his money back, but after I found out about Gabriel's suicide..."

"You felt guilty."

"What would you have done?"

"The same thing," Ally said. "So you think Gabriel's come back for revenge?"

Nora nodded slowly. "But through... *Lucy?*"

"What else did she... *he* say?"

"Horrible things." Nora spoke in a whisper. "I'm afraid to repeat it, and I'm not sure I can do this anymore, Ally. I thought I could just ignore it, but it's not going away—it's getting worse."

Ally studied her for a long moment, then stepped forward and touched her shoulder. "We'll take a break. I know you just got here, but you need to cool down. This is some heavy shit. I'll close up the parlor now."

Nora shook her head. "I can't afford to take any more time off."

"Well, you need a break," Ally said firmly. "Go grab a coffee. I'll watch Blanco. Don't worry about a thing."

The thought of coffee *was* appealing. "Are you sure?"

"You deserve it." Ally glanced back at Blanco's carrier. "I got this. Take all the time you need."

Nora nodded slowly and took a deep breath. "Yes," she said. "You're right."

"Of course, I am."

"I'll get some pet supplies too."

"Do you know what you need?" Ally asked.

She did, but she couldn't think straight. Her mind kept jumping back to what had happened in the séance room with Lizzie, and what Lucy had said.

Ally seemed to sense her indecision and walked to the front desk. "I'll make a list." She wrote a few things on a scratchpad, then handed it to Nora. "This should be enough for now."

Nora glanced at the list but couldn't focus on it. Looking up, she met her sister's gaze. "Something's wrong, Ally. Something has *changed*."

The concern on Ally's face deepened. "I feel it too. When you get back, we'll talk."

❦ 21 ❦

Nora pushed open the parlor's door and stepped inside. The bell above the door jingled, but then it was quiet. The front desk was empty.

Had Ally also stepped away for a coffee? Taking off her coat, a soft fluttering noise came from somewhere in the back, accompanied by Ally's unmistakable laugh.

Stepping toward the noises, Nora followed the laughter until she found Ally sitting cross-legged on the floor in the break room. Her sister's auburn hair was loose and frazzled, and a grin lit up her freckled face. Blanco sat in Ally's outstretched arms, and she was cradling him like a baby.

The cat's unblinking eyes fixed on Nora, and she froze.

"Ally," she said, "why is he out of his carrier?"

Ally looked up, unbothered. "He looked bored in there, poor guy. He has to stretch his legs sometime."

Nora looked at the carrier in the corner, its door sitting wide open. "You know he's been acting strangely since yesterday. Lucy..." Lucy's face flashed through her mind, the way Blanco had licked her daughter's neck and bared his teeth. She wanted to drop down, scoop him up, and toss him back in the carrier at that moment, although she had bigger things to focus on. She swallowed hard.

"He's okay." Ally brushed his fur, starting from his neck, pausing near his scars, and down to the tip of his tail.

"Fine," Nora said. "Just don't let him out of your sight."

Ally smiled at him, stroked his fur again, then put him back in the carrier anyway. "A beautiful white cat like this is hard to miss. What's the deal with his scars?"

Nora glanced down at the carrier before answering. "His owner... abused him."

"Gabriel?" A flash of pain swept over Ally's face. "That's awful. Why would anyone do something like that?"

Gabriel's furious face flashed through Nora's mind, but she pushed it away. "He did it before killing himself."

Ally groaned again. "Heartless."

Nora waited until Ally closed Blanco's carrier door before saying, "I need your help."

"With what?" Ally stood and brushed the loose fur off her clothes.

"This is going to sound weird coming from me, but I think... we need to do a séance."

The words hung in the air between them, and Ally's face showed a bit of confusion as she walked out of the room toward the front desk while glancing around. "Did someone come in?"

Nora followed her. "Not with a customer."

"Oh, I didn't think I heard anyone." Ally stopped and met her gaze. "A séance for who?"

"For me. We need to communicate with Gabriel."

Her sister's eyes widened. "A real séance?"

"A real one. No theatrics, no gimmicks. I need this one to actually work."

Ally's eyes gleamed with curiosity. "Are you serious about this?"

"What choice do I have?" Nora asked. "I didn't believe it, at first, but... things can't go on like this."

Ally nodded slowly, then a little faster. "Now you're talking my language. I've got just the thing."

Nora followed her to the back room with a knot in her stomach. If anyone could make sense of all the recent strange events, it was Ally.

The cluttered mess in the back room was overwhelming, yet it all somehow made sense to Ally. Her sister moved through it with ease, unfazed by the mess. The shelves were stuffed with old books, jars of herbs, and boxes of trinkets, along with decades of their family's bookkeeping in well-labeled banker's boxes. Stepping to the back corner, her sister stopped at a leather-bound book and pulled it off the shelf. A bit of dust followed it as she carried it back to the séance table and opened it with great care. The pages were brittle and yellowed with age.

"This," Ally said, "*this* is the real deal. Victorian spiritualists, ancient rites, occult practices, you name it—it's all in here."

They sat down across from each other. Her sister flipped through the pages as if she'd only read the book yesterday. The pages smelled of old books—the unmistakable smell of authenticity. Ally stopped on one page filled with diagrams and scrawled handwriting, and she pointed to one paragraph.

"This is what I'm talking about here. They used to do this back in the early spiritualist movement—one of the classic methods, not the type of thing we do now. It doesn't have any of the flair and theatrics that your clients expect, although they used some of the same techniques back then too. This one is old school. You need to draw a circle on the floor. Chalk works best, but salt can do in a pinch. Candles at the cardinal points and something personal to communicate with the spirit you're trying to contact. *That's* the key." She tapped the page again as if to show its importance. "You'll need something the spirit was connected to in life, something they owned and cherished."

Nora nodded, trying to take in everything her sister had just said. This wasn't pretend anymore. It was as if she'd played air guitar for years in front of a cheering audience, and then someone had thrust a real guitar into her hands for the first time. Now she was expected to play an actual song without practicing. "Do you know how to do all those things?"

She nodded. "I do."

"Do you think you can guide me through the process?"

"Of course," Ally said. "I've had your back all my life, remember?"

"I couldn't have done it without you. This won't be like putting on a performance for a client, so we should focus on what we can control." Nora glanced around the room. "The circle, the candles, the personal object. We'll need to get those things as soon as possible."

Ally nodded, flipping through more pages. "We'll need to be very precise about this. Any mistake and we could invite the wrong things in."

Nora swallowed. "Father Tony said the same thing. What sort of *wrong things* are we talking about?"

"Imagine your worst nightmare coming to life," Ally said. "That pretty much nails it."

A chill ran down Nora's spine. "Then we won't make any mistakes, will we?"

"Definitely not," Ally said. She grabbed a notebook from a ledge nearby and started scribbling notes in it. They worked together to map out exactly what they would do, the objects that they would need, where they would place them, and how they were to be used. Ally considered the situation from every angle. After only a short time, they had pieced their plan together, except for one thing.

"We need something that belonged to Gabriel," Ally said. "A watch or a shirt or a photo. Something that he cherished."

Blanco's copper eyes flashed through Nora's mind. "I know just the thing."

$\maltese$ 22 $\maltese$

Nora skimmed through another worn leather book that Ally had pulled from a shelf. She turned the pages slowly, careful not to damage the brittle paper. Many of the pages were loose or torn, and everything smelled of mildew.

The two of them sat side by side at the long oak table, one of the discarded antiques left behind from her family's business. The storage room had become a graveyard of her family's memories after her mother had passed away six years earlier. It was cramped and stuffy, but Ally had set up a small library in one corner, gathering up all the stray books in the building and placing them neatly on shelves where they might actually be used, even bringing in some of her own.

After returning from college, Ally had gone above and beyond to organize things. Her sister was proficient in every area of the business—marketing, finance, design, cleaning, and customer relations—and their skills complemented each other perfectly. Nora handled the front end, while Ally handled the back end.

She'd taken the reins of the business with genuine enthusiasm, fueled by her sister's infectious energy, but now that fire had faded to a dying ember, and she couldn't help but wonder if the family business would even survive another year.

While she pretended to be engrossed in the text, Ally tried to explain to her the ancient rituals of séances dating back to the Victorian years of the spiritualists and even hundreds of years earlier. It was hard to concentrate on the flurry of information Ally was presenting, and every few minutes, a noise came through the wall separating them from her father. He was likely dozing in his recliner, but if he'd wandered into the storage room at that moment and saw them "messing around," he would most likely scold them for wasting time instead of being out front in the parlor.

"We shouldn't be doing this here," Nora said, her voice barely above a whisper.

Ally followed Nora's gaze, closed the book, and said, "What choice do we have?"

Nora nodded slowly. Her sister was right. They had everything they needed for the séance right there. She opened the book again as Ally flipped a page and continued skimming the text. The terminology and words made no sense to her, but she tried to grasp at least the concepts that Ally was presenting. Her sister had a warehouse of knowledge stuffed in that brain of hers, and she seemed to know the subject better than anyone.

Ally hesitated, then set the book aside and straightened in her chair. "Would you like to start now?"

Nora clenched her teeth. "Shouldn't we practice a little more? Do a trial run?"

"There's no such thing as a trial run for a medium," Ally said. "It either happens or it doesn't."

"You've done this before though, right?"

"Never," Ally said. "I mean, it's all theoretical, and each medium has their own way of interacting with the spirits. Some people are psychic and some aren't, like you and me. But the books explain how to do it, so let's just try it and see what happens."

Nora swallowed. "Yes, let's do it."

They stood, gathered a few books, and walked to the séance room. Taking her place at the head of the table, Nora looked to Ally for instruction. "What's the process?"

"I've got it here." Ally sat across from Nora, in the seat where her clients normally did, and reached for a notebook where she had carefully written down the steps in an easy-to-understand form. "Alright, first step, cleanse the space. We did that this morning, but I'll do it again." She pulled a small bundle of sage from a shelf, lit it with a match, blew it out, and waved the smoking herb through the air. "We light this, letting the smoke fill the room. It's supposed to clear out any bad energy."

"This whole place is full of bad energy." Nora gestured to some chalk beside Ally's notebook. "And the chalk?"

"This is to draw the circle on the floor that I mentioned. It's supposed to protect us from whatever we're inviting into this place." Ally paused and looked into Nora's eyes. "Are you getting cold feet?"

Nora shrugged. "You think this will actually work? I mean... seriously?"

"There's no guarantee, I suppose."

Nora looked away, lighting the candle at the center of the table. "I'm not afraid," she said. "Gabriel left us no choice, didn't he? And he's not going to stop unless we face him."

Ally continued the process of lighting more sage, then picked up the chalk and began sketching a circle on the floor around the séance table. Almost immediately, the room dropped several degrees colder. Either the air conditioner had kicked into high gear or the furnace had switched off, letting the cool outside air rush in.

"He's here," Nora said.

Ally looked around as if she might see him. "We've got to pick up the pace a little, that's all."

The sage burned slowly, sending a column of smoke spiraling into the air. It reminded Nora too much of what had happened in the room that morning, so she swept her hand through it to break it up.

Ally finished drawing the circle on the floor. It was more than a simple circle, as Ally had copied an image from one of the books with five points around the circle marked with symbols at each point, their meaning completely unknown to her.

If this had been a séance for a customer and Ally had drawn the design, Nora would have confidently launched into a well-rehearsed performance, weaving an elaborate explanation full of meaningless but convincing and mystical phrases and jargon she'd absorbed over the years. But now, as she sat there watching Ally work with calm certainty, Nora felt like an imposter in her own parlor.

For once, she wasn't the one in control.

She understood the craft well enough but had never studied it the way Ally had. Her father had pushed her just enough to make it look convincing, and in his eyes, she excelled. She could talk the talk but never had reason to push herself further. The family always supplied the answers, while Ally was the one left doing all the homework.

After Ally finished with the chalk, she stood and observed her work while folding her arms over her chest. "That looks good."

"Is that everything?" Nora asked.

Ally's eyes went wide. "Oh, I almost forgot!" She darted out of the room and came back holding Blanco's carrier. She placed him in the corner, and the cat faced them directly. His eyes seemed to pierce her with a knowing of what she was planning to do.

"Tell your owner to come back to us," Nora said to Blanco in a soft tone. "I want to apologize."

Blanco meowed and stared at Ally as she worked to light all the candles.

"I think Blanco knows what we're planning," Nora said.

Ally glanced over at him and seemed to study his face.

"Gabriel has a deep connection to his cat, maybe from branding him. The symbol is obviously occult. It only makes sense that their connection extends into the afterlife."

"Let's hope it's enough to pull him in."

Ally sat again, then started reading the incantation out loud, and Nora mouthed the words while adjusting the lit candle at the center of the table. They had practiced the lines several times over the last hour in the storage room, but now she couldn't remember most of it. "You're going to have to actually say the words," she said. "No pretending this time."

Nora nodded and shifted in her seat to get a better view of the text that filled an entire page. "It's a lot to digest."

"I'll guide you, but we should both say it," Ally said. "More power. Put your heart into it like you do for every customer that comes in."

"It's not the same."

"It *is* the same, just that the intentions are different. Say it like you mean it."

They rehearsed the incantation again, with Nora repeating the words out loud this time.

The candles flickered, and Nora's heart skipped a beat.

"Did you feel that?" Ally asked.

Nora nodded. The room had grown even colder, and she had the sense that someone was watching them. Blanco let out another meow.

Turning her face up, Nora spoke. "Can you hear me, Gabriel? We have Blanco with us, and I know you want to talk."

The candles trembled in their holders. The flames bent sideways as if a gust of wind had caught them. Nora squeezed her hands into fists to keep them from trembling.

The door to the séance room creaked open. A puff of warmer air swept in, mixed with the smell of menthol cigarettes.

Her father appeared in the doorway. "What the hell is this?"

✺   23   ✺

Their father appeared in the doorway and glanced around the room. His gaze stopped at the candle, the books on the table, Blanco, and then down to the chalk circle surrounding the table. Despite the hallway light casting a shadow over his face, she could see his piercing gaze and his expression darkened.

Nora considered her options. She could switch into performance mode to lighten the mood, explaining their odd behavior as just 'testing out new technology,' but he would see through that. "Dad, I am—"

He glanced at his watch and then down the hallway toward the front door. "It's 10 a.m. and you're sitting in here playing games? Where's the client? All the lights are off up there. You closed the shop up early for this? For this nonsense?"

"It's not nonsense," Nora said firmly. "You don't understand."

He stepped into the room and stared at Ally. "Oh, I understand plenty. What's she gotten you to believe this week? That you're actually going to perform a real séance? Who are you planning to bring back, your mom?"

"That's hurtful, Dad," Nora said. "Don't bring Mom into this."

"She failed to raise you right, and you never listened to me."

"Stop," Nora said.

"I thought all this time you were in here with a client, but instead, you're just wasting time."

Ally pulled her books toward her, as if he might take them away.

"Just go back into your room and leave us alone," Nora said. "We need to fix something."

"You're the ones who need to be fixed."

Nora's face warmed. He was glaring at Ally, and it was clear he was a breath away from telling her to leave forever. She couldn't stay silent for a moment longer. "I'm not perfect, you know, and neither was Mom. This is *our* business now, remember? You handed over the keys to us—so just get the hell out of here. You're the one who told me to do whatever it takes—"

"Not this!" her father shouted. "You're not supposed to—I set up everything for you both. You've got everything here to launch a successful career."

"Like you and Mom? We barely had enough money to fix the front window, Dad. How is that success?"

"It is what you make of it. Maybe you would succeed if you weren't pissing your time away, sitting in the corner like some little girl playing dress-up."

The candles in the room suddenly flared, and Ally gasped. The table rattled, and Blanco retreated to the back of his carrier. One of the mirrors on the wall shattered, leaving a web of cracks that radiated from the center.

Her father's face went pale. "What the hell?"

Nora didn't answer. The temperature in the room plummeted. Her mouth dropped open, and she could see her breath. Folding her arms over her chest to stay warm, an unmistakable presence had entered the room.

Her father backed away, pointing to the circle on the floor. "No, no."

A moment later, the candles went out. He turned to leave,

but the door slammed shut before he reached it, and the room went dark.

The sound of their heavy breathing grew louder. Ally switched on her phone and used it in flashlight mode to find her way to the matches near the candle. Lighting the candle in the center of the table first, she went around and lit the others before turning back toward them.

"Do you feel that?" Ally asked.

"I do," Nora said.

Someone was standing with them in the darkness. Ally switched on her phone in flashlight mode, and Nora's body tensed. She hoped they wouldn't find anyone, but at the same time, she longed to get it over with.

When the light passed over Blanco's carrier, she caught a glimpse of the cat's copper eyes. He was pressing his head against the bars of the carrier with that same smug grin, staring out at something unseen, his eyes fixed on a corner of the room where Ally hadn't yet searched.

"Over there," Nora pointed to where Blanco was staring with a fixed gaze.

Ally followed her gaze, turning toward the corner and lighting it up, although nothing they could see was there. No sign of Gabriel. Nora gasped in a deep breath and focused her eyes on the spot.

"This is ridiculous," her father said. "You're wasting your time with this nonsense. You can do better than this, Nora. Am I the target this time? A parlor trick just for me? Don't waste your time. This is the cheap stuff customers hate. They'll never buy it."

Despite his insults, Nora kept her gaze on the corner where she sensed someone staring back at her. "Not this time," she said in a soft voice.

A dark mass shifted and Nora jumped back, letting out a little scream. She turned and Ally focused her light on the air behind her. "He's here."

"Who's here?" her father asked.

"Gabriel," Ally answered.

"Who the hell is Gabriel?"

Nora ignored him, pointing into the darkness as the shadow suddenly rose to the ceiling. "He's moving."

"Who's moving?" her father asked. "You can stop your little game. I'm not impressed."

"We don't care if you're impressed, Dad. This is the real thing. Sit down and shut up or leave."

He did neither. He folded his arms over his chest with his chin up and grumbled under his breath.

Nora focused on Blanco. The cat's gaze seemed to follow the same shadow while pacing frantically in its carrier. "Why can't we see him?"

"Do you really want that?" Ally asked.

"Not really."

Slipping back into her seat at the table, Ally clutched Nora's hands again and switched off her phone's screen. The single candle's light was enough for now.

Nora turned back to her father. "Sit," she said, "or leave."

He grumbled a few more words but obeyed, dropping into a chair beside the door. The legs scraped across the floor, the harsh noise filling the room and breaking the silence. Nora closed her eyes and clutched Ally's hands tighter. She mumbled some of the words she'd forgotten, hoping it might help to keep the energy alive.

The cold air chilled her face and arms, and she shivered. Her father shifted in his chair and let out a heavy sigh. No doubt, it was intended as an insult.

Even with her eyes closed, she could see the candlelight faintly glowing through her eyelids. The flames were flickering in the stillness.

"Is there more to your act, or are we finished?" her father asked.

Nora ignored him and instead called out, "Gabriel, are you here?"

Only silence.

"If you're here, show yourself," she said. "We need to talk to you about what happened."

Nora opened her eyes halfway. The flames were flickering wildly, almost violently.

Ally was also peeking around the room. "Nora?" she whispered in a cautious tone. "Keep talking to him."

Their father chuckled nervously. "Clever trick with the candle, but this is all the standard stuff. Show me something *bold*!"

Something knocked against the bottom of the table.

Ally's knee? Nervously bouncing or shivering against it. But then it grew louder, even as Ally stared back at her and met her gaze.

Nora swallowed. "Gabriel. We're here to listen. Speak to us."

The knocking grew louder, like someone frantically pounding their fists to get inside. Ally's eyes grew wider, and her lips were quivering. She was mumbling something under her breath. A prayer?

"That's enough, Nora," her father said in a wavering voice. "Shut it down."

"I can't," Nora snapped back. She glanced at him for the first time since they'd started. There was fear in his eyes, and a pang of guilty delight swept through her at seeing him afraid for once. "I have to finish this."

"Stop!" he yelled while struggling to open the door. It wouldn't budge.

The knocking stopped suddenly, and the room fell silent. Nora gasped in a breath, but only a moment later, the table started trembling. It *was* rigged to move on command, but Ally hadn't triggered it this time. The rumbling started slowly at first, then grew more violent.

The table lurched from side to side, cracking its legs against the floor. Nora grabbed the obsidian mirror, and only a moment later, the candle toppled over, rolled off the table's edge, and hit the floor with a dull thud. Ally grabbed the book and cradled it in her arms.

Their father swore under his breath. "Nora, stop this nonsense!"

Within the darkness, Nora could still see her father's terrified gaze locked onto her while he clawed at the empty air. He, too, had seen something.

She didn't respond, instead squeezing the mirror tighter until the cascading violence came to a halt and the table crashed to the floor. The room held its breath.

Glancing down into the mirror, the light from Ally's phone reflected off its black surface. A fog swept over the glass, and an outline started to take shape. A face emerged—Gabriel's face. He looked nothing like the distraught man who had stormed out of her parlor a month earlier. Now his skin was black, stretched tight against his bony structure, his hair waving slowly in the air. His eyes were gaping dark voids.

"You called me," he said.

Except his voice didn't come from the mirror. It came from somewhere behind them. Nora turned around to face her father, except he'd dropped to the floor, sitting with his back against the door, his face drained of color. He looked up and met her gaze. A twisted grin spread across his face. Gabriel's grin.

"How does it feel, Nora?" her father spoke in a voice low and guttural, not his own. "How does it feel to lose someone you love?"

"Dad!" Nora screamed.

Clutching at his chest, his eyes rolled up into his head, and his mouth fell open. He slumped forward until his body started to convulse.

Nora jumped out of her chair and reached for him. Ally did the same, rushing to his side.

"We have to get him to the hospital," Nora shouted.

"How does it feel?" Her father's teeth chattered violently.

Ally grabbed a towel from the coffee table and stuffed it between his teeth to keep him from biting down on his tongue. Stepping back, she switched on the lights and dialed 911.

Nora held her father tighter, even as his body convulsed violently against her. He was still breathing, but she struggled to keep him steady. It was all she could do to keep him from hurting himself.

Using her shoe, Ally smeared through the circle of chalk, closing the door to the spirit world. But it was too late.

With the lights on, the air warmed again slowly. While they waited for an ambulance, Nora spotted Blanco through the bars of the carrier across the room. He let out a meow and then licked his paws.

24

Their father was dead.

Nora knew it the second he'd hit the floor.

They'd done their best to revive him before the medics arrived, giving him CPR for several agonizing minutes without success, and Ally had even taken over the chest compressions when Nora's arms ached too much and exhaustion had set in. But her father had never regained consciousness. All their efforts had failed.

Still, she held out hope as the paramedics arrived. There was something in the way they rushed to his side, unpacked a slew of equipment, and checked him over frantically that brightened her heart. Maybe there was still something they could do. Maybe it wasn't too late.

But her heart sank when they admitted he was gone and lifted him onto a stretcher, his lifeless body shrouded beneath a white sheet.

It was strange seeing her father like that. This was the man who had made every major decision in her life, and now he was silent and would never make another decision for her ever again.

It was strange.

Surreal.

One of the medics came over and spoke in a soft voice. "We'll transport your father to the county morgue. You can make arrangements with the funeral home of your choice, and they'll coordinate with the coroner's office to release the body. Do you need their contact information?"

Nora barely nodded, and he slipped a piece of paper into her trembling fingers. There was just a simple address on it, nothing else.

And then everybody left.

That was it.

No time to process the moment. No questions, no suspicions, no accusations or consequences. They just all walked out of there with her father's body, and she was left to grasp the finality of watching them put him into the back of the ambulance and close the doors.

The red and blue flashing lights from the emergency vehicles pulsed across the streets, and sirens blared before the ambulance pulled away. A moment later, everyone was gone.

Her father was gone.

Ally's voice cut through the silence. "Did you call Daniel yet?"

"Not yet."

"I'll drive you home."

Nora turned to face her sister, trying to wrap her head around the question. Where was her home? At the parlor? With Daniel and Lucy? She seemed paralyzed in the moment, and let out a small, bitter laugh. "He's dead because of me."

Ally took a step closer, her eyes red with tears. "You don't know that."

"Don't I? You heard what he said, right?"

"Yes," Ally said softly.

"I know it was Gabriel talking through him, but it *was* my fault. That wasn't just a heart attack from a lifetime of cigarettes, fast food, and drinking. Yes, maybe it would have happened at some point, but I flipped the switch."

Ally let out a slow breath, rubbing her arms. "Whatever happened in there, you can't blame yourself."

Nora shivered and wrapped her arms across her chest. The chilly winter air filled the front room. "I pushed it too far. I thought I could control it." She squeezed her eyes shut. Within the darkness, she could still see her father's terrified gaze locked onto her while he clawed at the empty air in his last moments. He, too, had seen something. "I should be in that ambulance instead of him," Nora whispered. "How am I going to live with this?"

Ally exhaled slowly. "Listen to me. You didn't kill him. Whatever harmed him... it was already here. He just got in the way."

"He got between me and whatever the hell I brought into this world," Nora said bitterly.

"We were only doing what we thought was right."

"We shouldn't have done this." Nora shook her head. "Not alone. We should have gotten help. Professional help."

"From whom?"

"From... anyone." Nora squeezed herself tighter. "I can't do this anymore."

Ally gave a sympathetic nod.

Nora glanced around the parlor, staring at the antique woodwork. All the renovations her father had meticulously worked on to restore the place. The history and emotions seemed to suffocate her. She used to love this place, but now it felt like a coffin. "I need to get out of here," she said. "Not just the parlor, but everything. The séances, the business, the lies..."

"Then that's what we should do," Ally said.

The honesty in her sister's voice startled her. No arguments, no trying to convince her otherwise. Despite their three-year age gap, Ally had always been the one to see the bigger picture, to recognize the deeper meanings when Nora couldn't see past the surface. Her sister frowned with a bit of fear in her eyes—their father's death had shaken her too.

"I'll take care of everything," Ally said. "I'll close up for the night. You need to be with Daniel and Lucy."

Nora shook her head. "No, I want to stay here... for now. You go home."

Ally studied her. "Are you sure? I don't mind staying if you want me to."

"I need some time to think," she said softly. "Go home, little sis... I'll call you tomorrow."

Ally didn't argue. "Okay, but just say the word, and I'll be there."

"I know you will. That's what I love about you." Nora nodded and stared at the floor. The weight of everything pressed down on her, but she needed to be alone in that moment.

"I love you, too." Ally hesitated a moment longer before putting on her coat and heading toward the front door. When she left, the chime of the bell above the door rang on her way out.

When the door clicked shut, Nora took a deep breath and the silence flooded in around her. How could she have thought, even for a moment, that she could successfully communicate with the dead? Had arrogance twisted her mind after so many years of pretending? She was an actor, a fraud, and she had paid a heavy price for believing that she was someone special.

As she stood motionless within the crushing isolation, the sound of someone breathing came from across the room—not someone, but some *thing*.

Blanco.

Ally had let him out of the carrier earlier to use the litter box and hadn't put him back. Nora turned to face him. He was perched at the end of the counter with that same smug look on his face. Had he watched them the whole time? She'd forgotten he was still there, his eyes gleaming in the dim light of the parlor. His tail was curled neatly around his paws and he sat motionless. He was staring at her, and the corners of his mouth were tilted upward in a little grin. Was he holding back laughter? Did he know something she didn't?

Nora stepped to the front door and flipped the sign over the door to "CLOSED." The tears welled up in her eyes. Wiping away a tear, more followed, and a moment later she was openly weeping. She faced away from Blanco. It was better not to give him the satisfaction of seeing her cry.

25

Nora walked to the back of the parlor and paused at the open door to the séance room. It was empty now, and the lights were off. Still, the looming darkness filled her with dread. Her father had died in that space on the floor. How could she ever go in there again without remembering what had happened?

How does it feel?

Even though they hadn't come from *him*, his final words had stung. Her father was never one to hold back, but nothing about his death was normal. In his dying breath before collapsing, he'd lashed out at her. Not "I love you," not a plea for help, not regret, but biting words intended to rip her heart out.

How does it feel?

Her father hadn't said those words, but still they stabbed at her heart. Someone had consumed him long enough to push those words up from his throat as he'd gasped for his last breath.

All just to teach her a lesson.

Gabriel's voice.

How does it feel?

"It feels awful," she said into the shadows. Her heart ached.

Was Gabriel still there, watching her from somewhere just

out of sight, waiting for just the right moment to catch her off guard and do the same to her?

"You'll never get another chance," she said, "because I quit. I'm done. Whatever pain I caused you, I'm sorry. You took Dad's life—you got what you wanted—so now we're even. Get the hell out of my life."

She shut the door with a little more force than necessary, then turned down the hallway toward her father's apartment in the back.

Everything seemed different now, pointless. Where was her father's gruff voice? His heavy footfalls? His absence should have made her feel better—she wouldn't have to listen to any of it ever again—but instead, the silence had knocked the wind out of her.

Opening the door to his apartment, she stood at the threshold and stared inside at the mess he'd left behind. A monument to his chaotic life. There were old books teetering in stacked piles, a worn recliner with cigarette burns in the armrest, and an ashtray overflowing on the coffee table despite her constant nagging for him to empty it.

The glow from a desk lamp was the only thing warm in that place. How had she grown up in such an environment? How had her father let everything fall apart after her mother died?

Nora had tried to keep his space clean to the best of her abilities over the years, but he hadn't appreciated her efforts. Nothing had seemed to matter to him, not his apartment nor himself. The mess was a snapshot of how far he had fallen in recent months, and now it was frozen in time.

Nora swallowed and stepped inside. The floor creaked as she made her way around the room, taking a long look at things she had never truly noticed before. His oak desk sat in the corner, stuffed with loose papers, bills, and mail he had failed to throw away. There were also piles of boxes he'd kept over the years, some of them labeled: ledgers, client records, taxes. Somehow, he'd kept the business running smoothly despite his chaotic methods, pushing her forward like a drill sergeant pushing a new recruit who always seemed to fall behind. He'd been the force behind everything in their parlor, his empire of smoke and mirrors, who had trained her almost daily in their early years to see grief as a business model instead of what it really was.

Despite everything he had pushed on her, somehow…

She exhaled as the realization caught her off guard. She wasn't crying or devastated, or even sad.

She was numb.

Everything inside was numb, yes, but she also felt relieved. Relieved that she no longer had to put up with his endless bullshit, relieved that she could finally breathe without the constant criticism streaming through the doorway. Even now, his words came back to her: "You can't let them out of the door until you've made the sale. Push the emotions, Nora. Push the buttons that get them crying."

A pang of guilt swept through her chest. Her heart ached for her father, yes, but even more for her clients. Was that wrong? Her father was gone forever, and part of her was glad. A bitter laugh escaped her lips.

I'm a terrible daughter.

No wonder her dad had encouraged her to develop her talent for manipulating others. She was *so good* at it.

A natural.

She had a skill—an amazing talent—to switch off her feelings as easily as turning off a light. It was all just acting, taking on the role of compassionate medium, gateway to the dead. An A-list performer deserving of an Oscar for her years of achievements, and everything she had done had been only to please him.

Who would she please now?

The room grew colder. A chill traced a line across the back of her neck, and she froze, her fingers gripping the edge of a chair near the desk. It tickled the back of her head and then faded in an instant as if a spiderweb had brushed against her skin on the way down.

The furnace kicked out warm air from a vent near the floor, and the rush of air fluttered a stack of papers. At the same time, something rattled behind her. Turning toward the sound, her father's bedroom door drifted open a few inches and then stopped.

The wet sound of someone swallowing and the smell of menthol cigarettes filled the air. Her father's door shifted again, opening wider until it came to a halt against the doorjamb. The light seeping in through the half-open blinds lit his bedroom well enough to see that his mess extended into every corner. A bottle of alcohol lay on the floor just inside the door with a wide stain across the carpet—a fresh stain.

While staring into his room, someone's arm reached down and lifted the bottle off the floor, pulling it out of her view as if trying to hide it from her.

Her heart raced faster as she took a sharp breath. "Is someone here?"

A shadow passed over the floor, yet the figure remained out of sight. A wet kiss sound broke the silence, like someone finishing a drink, and the liquid splashing back to the bottom of a bottle before it hit the floor again and rolled out toward the open doorway.

Nora stepped back. She could call for help. Ally, Daniel, or the police could arrive within minutes. Someone had gotten inside. Maybe her father had left the back door unlocked while dealing with the chaos in the front room.

A shadow emerged again on the floor, forming the silhouette of a man as it filled the doorway and stopped. But instead of revealing an intruder, the shadow stood alone among the debris. Just a dark shape without a source, it flowed across the carpet, over the now empty bottle, and out of the bedroom toward her. It moved in slow strides, its path wavering at times, until it reached the recliner and settled into the space where her father had spent so many hours of his life.

"Dad?" She held her breath as the shadow gathered and swelled, distorting into a murky, shifting mass as if his entire body had been stripped away, leaving nothing but a lingering cloud of cigarette smoke in its place.

It was him. She could tell by the way he tilted his head and draped his hands over the armrests. This was her father, but his eyes were now hollow pits, dark and consuming. He glanced toward her with his mouth hanging open far too wide, as if he was trying to say something but had forgotten how. A billow of smoke plumed from somewhere down his throat, rising in thin wisps that spread out like a final cry for help.

She stumbled backward but couldn't look away. "Dad." Her voice barely left her throat. "Is that you?"

Another shadow rose from behind his recliner, a darker silhouette peeking up from behind him. A man—first his blackened eyes, his gaunt face, then his extended neck, stretching thin and crooked from the top of his smoky wardrobe.

Gabriel.

He stepped out from behind the recliner and threw his clawed hand across her father's head, scraping his nails over his skin. Her father stirred in his seat, lifting forward as if to rise, until Gabriel thrust him back.

Gripping her father's head like a melon with the tips of his fingernails, he swung her father's face toward her.

"Daddy's here." Her father spoke in a voice not his own, and his dead stare missed her gaze. "Sit with me, my little liar. Tell me all your sins."

Another shadow emerged from behind the recliner. The imposing outline of an animal—a dog. A puff of smoke billowed from its nostrils. A pit bull. Its enormous black eyes and smoky appearance formed twisted features. It came around the side of the recliner, slowly transforming into something almost solid, its movements jerking unnaturally.

Two more dogs emerged in the same way, one of them gaunt and tall, a Doberman pinscher, and the other only slightly smaller, a German shepherd, as threatening as the others, and joined it a moment later. All three of them had a strange symbol branded into the side of their flesh. The pit bull turned toward her as another puff of smoke billowed from its nostrils out to the sides like an angry bull ready to charge. Inching toward her, its breath rattled like a broken pipe as it crept forward.

She tried to turn away, even just to look away, but the ghastly sight kept her paralyzed with fear, even as the pit bull lurched at her. A thick darkness poured from its mouth, billowing black smoke as if its lungs were fueled by the fires of hell. The smoke soon obscured everything around them as it rushed at her with full force.

With a jolt, she turned and screamed, scrambling toward the door with her heart racing. If only she could close it in time...

The icy air darkened around them. A bit of the smoke swept into her gaping mouth and dropped into her lungs. The sickening stench filled her nose and throat, cutting off her air as she pushed out into the hallway. She gasped for air until the door slammed shut behind her, cutting off the smoke from the rest of the parlor.

Deafening barks and growls exploded from behind her, but she didn't stop to look back. The door rattled and then cracked under the weight of the dogs but it held.

She couldn't stop. Not until she stood outside on the sidewalk, with the icy evening air biting at her bare skin. The traffic and gentle wind snapped her out of the nightmare, and she took in a deep breath, coughing out the last of the smoke as reality flooded in around her.

Turning back to face the parlor, she shivered. Nobody was behind her—no dogs, not Gabriel, not her father—and the smoke was gone. Nothing moved inside the parlor except a white object barely shifting within the shadows.

Blanco.

He crept into view and pressed his paws against the glass in the door, but it had latched shut when she'd run outside. His peering eyes stared back at her.

Hate rose in her chest. As crazy as it seemed, the cat had something to do with her father's death. It was Gabriel's cat, after all. How could she bring him home to Lucy ever again? Somehow, this was *his* fault.

She wanted him gone. Forever.

The answer was simple. Just a little turn of the handle, pull the door open, and...

He wanted to go outside anyway. Why not let him run free and rid him from her life? Let someone else adopt him. A beautiful white cat like that would get picked up in no time.

She stepped toward the door but stopped. Lucy's pained face filled her mind. She could already hear her daughter's agonizing words when she returned home without him.

"Where's Blanco?" she would say.

The pain stabbed at her heart. No, she had to find a better way to handle this. She couldn't leave Blanco out in the cold.

Before she took another step, the door snapped open as if nudged by some unseen force. Blanco took advantage of the moment and bolted past her in a streak of white fur.

"Blanco, wait!"

It was too late. The door slammed shut again, and the cat had scrambled away around the side of the building.

She chased after him for several minutes, but the freezing air forced her to turn back inside.

Shivering inside the parlor, her heart sank. Lucy would be devastated, just as she'd imagined. How could she return home after everything that had happened? Her world had collapsed, and after a cautious glance around her parlor after stepping inside, she dropped into a chair behind the front desk and cried.

She folded her arms over her chest both to warm herself and to pull herself together. Someone would find Blanco. Someone would take him in and feed him and love him. Just not her child, not Lucy. It was better this way. The thought kept her from breaking down. No matter how much she wanted to pretend none of this was real, a small voice in her mind wouldn't let her.

Blanco had caused all of this.

It's better this way.

$\maltese$ 26 $\maltese$

Nora braced herself when she arrived home. She'd called Daniel just before leaving the parlor but had cut the call short with only a brief explanation about her father. He'd offered —insisted—to come get her, but she'd refused, convincing him it was better Lucy didn't find out tonight. Better to let her sleep. On her way home, Nora planned out everything she was going to say to him.

She found him reading a book in the living room when she stepped inside. When he met her gaze, the reality of everything sank in. Her father was gone, and she would never see him again. But even worse, her heart ached at the pain Lucy would feel after learning her grandfather had died. How would she tell her little girl the tragic news?

Daniel set the book down, stood, and walked to her, extending his arms just a bit. "How are you feeling?"

"Numb."

He embraced her cautiously at first until she sank into his arms. "I haven't told Lucy yet."

Nora tensed and then nodded. "That's good."

"I figured you'd want to tell her yourself," he said.

Nora pulled back a little. She stared into Daniel's eyes for answers. "How will I tell her? It all happened so fast."

Daniel didn't answer right away. He let out a slow breath and pulled her back in against him. "She'll get through it."

"She adored him," Nora said. "More than I ever did."

"It's a part of life, something she needs to learn."

Nora couldn't get her daughter's face out of her mind, picturing how Lucy would cry, maybe throughout the night, and she would ask a ton of questions about life and death and all that stuff Nora tried so hard to shield her from. "An eight-year-old shouldn't have to deal with talk of death."

"Do you want me to tell her?" Daniel asked.

Nora shook her head. "I'll do it, but it won't be easy."

Daniel pulled back and looked into her eyes. "Do you want to talk about it?"

"He had a heart attack." She glanced toward the floor. "At least, according to the paramedics."

"You have some doubts about that?"

"No," she said. "It makes sense, after the kind of life he lived."

He stared into her eyes for a long moment. "Something else bothering you?"

Blanco's hollow eyes flashed through Nora's mind, and she winced. "There's something I wish... something I can't get out of my mind. Blanco..."

Daniel's expression changed from concern to fear. "What happened to him?"

"He ran off."

"What do you mean he ran off?"

Nora glanced toward the stairs. She hoped her daughter's bedroom door was closed. "He ran out the door." She shook her head. "I tried to get him back but... He was gone before I had a chance to even grab my coat. His white fur blended in with the snow. I couldn't find him."

Daniel swallowed and rubbed the back of his neck. "Lucy... This is too much for a kid her age to deal with. I suppose we should go out there and search for him."

"I'm not sure I want to," she said.

"Why not?"

"It's hard to explain, Daniel. Something's not right with that cat."

"Are you talking about the bird he dragged in the other day? All cats do stuff like that. Like you said, it's in their nature."

"I know, but this one is... He's better off with someone else."

"Nora, Lucy can't lose two loved ones on the same day. It's too much. We have to go find him."

Nora shook her head. "You have to trust me. It's for the best."

Daniel looked into her eyes again as if trying to solve a riddle. How could she tell him about the way Blanco had stared at her after her father's death? The way the cat had smiled at her from across the room as if the whole thing was a joke? How could she explain the strange voice coming from Lucy in the backseat, and how Blanco had stared at her through it all? The disturbances— all of them—only happened when Blanco was around. He was no ordinary cat. Not in any sense of the word.

Daniel's expression darkened. "For the best?"

Her heart beat faster. "Please, just let it go for now," she said. "I'll tell her everything in the morning."

Daniel exhaled through his nose. He didn't push it, although he also glanced back in the direction of Lucy's room. "I hate this part of parenting."

"So do I." Nora's stomach twisted.

She wanted to tell him about everything she had experienced at the parlor, including the vision of her father's ghost. She could tell him everything, but he would insist that she was cracking under the pressure, a victim of her family's occult business. Of course, he would be there for her and would patiently listen to anything she had to say, but after all the years of fraudulently contacting the dead for profit, how could she possibly expect him to believe that she'd experienced something real? Was it delusions of a grieving mind? Daniel wouldn't judge her, but he also wouldn't believe her, and he wouldn't hesitate to repeat her promise to finally seek a new line of work. It all sounded crazy. That much was clear, and he might also suggest that she should seek professional help to deal with the trauma.

Daniel turned away. "Come to bed soon. You need to sleep."

Nora hesitated before trudging upstairs to bed. How would she even dare to close her eyes now with everything she'd witnessed?

After making herself comfortable under the sheets, she curled up to him, feeling the warmth of his body. She kept the lights on, and he didn't complain, or even say a word, although his expression showed he would stay up all night with her if she needed that.

At least she wasn't alone. Her mind flashed with a thousand images of everything she had witnessed that day: the catastrophic séance, her father's sudden death and haunting last words, and... Blanco's eyes.

Blanco.

What had gone wrong? Could she have done anything differently? Lucy would cry a lot in the morning. Her grandfather's death would be something she'd never forget, but the news of Blanco's disappearance would devastate her.

Staring across the room, she spotted a bit of frost along the bottom edge of the window glass. Blanco was out there in the freezing winter night... alone.

Someone would have found him by now.

You don't know that.

Someone would have seen him... with those big, beautiful... piercing eyes...

She shivered. Yes, the cat would have sought shelter in the

doorway of someone else's business by now, and they would have taken him in. A prized gift for someone else's child in someone else's family. It wasn't something she needed to worry about—it would all work out just fine in the end. And there was nothing more she could have done anyway.

No need to blame yourself for anything.

A gust of wind pushed against the glass, rattling the window-pane. Her eyes drooped a little as she lay motionless next to Daniel. Closing her eyes, the exhaustion started to kick in.

And then she heard it. A voice. Lucy's voice. It was so soft and distant she almost convinced herself that she'd imagined it. Then she heard it again.

"Come here," Lucy said.

Come here?

Nora's stomach dropped. The sickening, toxic weight filled her chest as she struggled to take in a breath. She bolted upright, her maternal instincts kicking in. Her pulse pounded in her ears as dread weighed her down.

"What's wrong?" Daniel asked.

Without turning around, she headed for the bedroom door. "You put Lucy to sleep, didn't you?"

"Yes..."

"I heard..."

"Heard what?"

Rushing out of the room, she charged down the hallway to Lucy's bedroom and threw her door open. The window sat wide open, and the room was freezing.

Lucy was there, beyond the window, sitting *outside* on the roof in her pajamas. She was extending her hand toward a white object on a tree branch a few feet in front of her beyond the edge of the roof.

Not an object—Blanco.

"Come here," Lucy called to him. "Be careful. Don't fall."

Panic shot through Nora's whole body. She charged to the

window and nearly threw herself onto the roof until Daniel gripped her arm to hold her back.

Blanco didn't budge. He looked like an oblong snowball perched on the branch, not an animal at all, until its black, empty eyes met Nora's gaze.

❧ 27 ❧

Nora's heart pounded. She wanted to jump out onto the roof and grab her daughter without the slightest thought of her own safety. If Daniel hadn't pulled her back in, she might have done exactly that.

"Lucy!" she called out while gripping the edge of the windowsill.

A gust of wind burst through the room, and some of Lucy's drawings fluttered into the air.

Daniel nudged her out of the way and charged ahead. Wearing only pajamas, he held one of Lucy's bedsheets with him and handed one end of it to Nora before jumping out the open window.

"Don't let go," he said.

She clutched it with all her strength.

Lucy was still trying to coax Blanco back inside. The cat was perched on a branch just out of reach, watching everything with a smug grin and a gleam of humor in its unblinking eyes.

He's pleased with himself. He knows exactly what he's doing.

"Blanco, you silly cat," Lucy said with outstretched arms. "What are you doing out there?"

"Lucy," Daniel called out in a soft tone, "don't move."

Her daughter looked back at him, watching him inch forward. "I have to save Blanco."

"Don't go out any further." He shook his head and gestured for her to come toward him.

"But he's going to fall," Lucy said in a panicked voice.

"He's not going to fall," Daniel reassured her. "I'll get him. Now let's get you back inside."

Lucy turned her focus back to Blanco, staring at him in the chilly air but holding her ground. "He's scared, Daddy. I have to help him."

"Lucy!" Nora yelled through the window. "Listen to me. Get back in here *right now*." Glancing down at the yard below, there were patches of snow to help break Lucy's fall if she slipped over the edge. But the driveway was covered in ice, and the sidewalk was straight down. She could easily break a few bones, or worse, if she landed wrong. The thought sent a chill up her spine.

"Lucy, grab my hand," Daniel called to her.

Another gust of wind ripped through the air between them. Lucy stretched out her hand toward the cat again, but still, Blanco didn't budge.

"Let him go," Daniel shouted.

Lucy let out an exasperated sigh and glanced back. "But he needs my help, Daddy." She spoke with such an innocent certainty, as if the solution was simple, and they just needed to open their eyes and understand.

Daniel inched forward on his knees, scraping them against the rough shingles. At least most of the snow and ice had melted away during a recent thaw. There was nothing to slow him down. "Sweetheart," he said, "I know you want to save him, but you have to come back inside now."

"No, no," Lucy shook her head and inched toward Blanco. "I can reach him."

"Lucy, stop!" Daniel yelled.

She stopped moving forward, and Daniel stretched out his

hand again. She took it this time. When her little hand touched his, he yanked her back toward the house.

For one terrifying second, Nora couldn't breathe. Lucy's foot slipped, and Daniel pulled her again. The sheet Nora held with both hands stretched tight at the same time, and she gripped it with all of her strength.

He yanked Lucy again, this time harder, and she let out a sharp, startled gasp, pulling her back toward him faster now. She seemed to surrender in his arms.

The tension in Nora's chest faded after Daniel maneuvered Lucy back inside through the window and her feet touched the floor. Daniel followed her a moment later, gasping for breath, and Nora slammed the window shut as soon as they were both out of the way.

She embraced her daughter's frigid body. Both of them were shivering uncontrollably. The cold wind was gone, although the chill still hung in the air. It was over. They were safe.

Lucy charged back to the window, even as Nora stood in the way. "Don't close it!"

Nora shifted to prevent her daughter from peering outside. "Let him go."

Lucy shook her head emphatically. "No, he'll freeze outside."

A rush of recognition swept through Nora. Her daughter had the same fierce determination, the same stubbornness to push past every warning sign in the face of danger. It was something Nora had learned in her life—that being stubborn didn't always save you. Sometimes it got you killed. "Lucy, he almost killed you."

"He didn't mean to, Mommy. You can't let him stay out there. He'll die."

Better him than you.

But she had no intention of letting Blanco freeze to death out there in front of Lucy. She turned to Daniel for an answer. He'd wrapped one of Lucy's other bedsheets around himself and was also shaking to stay warm. It was clear he was in no shape to climb up that tree to get Blanco down. The agonizing decision hung in the air. If she went outside to rescue that awful cat, would she really let him cozy up with her daughter again after all that had happened?

Lucy's pleas filled the air. She threw herself against Nora's legs and waist. "You can't let him die out there, Mommy. Please don't let him die."

The anger, exhaustion, and questions were too much to handle right now. How could she defend herself against Lucy's heartache? She couldn't say anything. Not now. How could she make a decision in that moment?

Lucy looked up at her with watering eyes. "Don't kill him, please."

Nora's gut twisted. She had to protect her daughter, but it would break her little heart to say no. It wasn't possible to refuse to help her. None of this was how she'd hoped things would go after her father's death. Lucy would also cry about that tomorrow. The exhaustion weighed on her. Lucy had already attached herself to Blanco, and it was clear that the cat had won.

"Daniel," she said without thinking. Glancing back out the window, Blanco was still there. "Can you try to coax Blanco back inside?"

Daniel went to the window and opened it, filling the room with another gust of freezing wind. Only a moment later, Blanco hopped off the branch onto the roof, his paws sliding a bit on the raw shingles, but he finally pranced inside a moment later. Daniel shut the window behind him.

It was that easy.

Lucy jumped to him, crying tears of joy. With a shake of his fur, he stretched out and then settled into her arms. "I'm so glad you're here with me, Blanco. Don't ever do that to me again. Don't you ever leave me again. You scared us."

28

Nora lifted Blanco out of Lucy's arms. "You can have him back in the morning," she said.

"Promise?" Lucy whispered.

Nora forced herself to give a little nod. Guilt swept through her as she squeezed Blanco in her arms, and he squirmed a bit. Keeping this cat in their home was a mistake. She had lied to Lucy to keep the peace, but how would she keep it in the morning? She had to get rid of him as soon as possible. What choice did she have? It was the right thing to do.

How could she *not* step in to protect Lucy from this... thing? It wasn't a cat—not really. At least, not anything *natural*. Something had gotten into it. Possessed by Gabriel's spirit? Or just his ghost whispering in its ear, guiding it all the way through the winter's darkness from her parlor back to her home? Something had gotten into it. No ordinary cat acted with such calculated malice.

She turned away quickly and carried Blanco out of the room before she lost her nerve, before Lucy had a chance to object. As soon as she stepped out into the hallway, the weight of everything crashed down on her.

Lucy could have died that night, and she would have lost two loved ones in a single day, all because of the creature now nestled snug in her arms. Blanco let out a deep, rhythmic purr and glanced around as if it were on an amusement ride. Nora tightened her grip on him and headed toward the laundry room before Lucy could say anything else.

Daniel shut Lucy's door behind her and came up behind Nora a moment later. "We'll need to keep an eye on her tonight. Make sure she doesn't sneak out and play with him again."

"I'm not worried about her," Nora said.

She walked to the laundry room and stepped inside. It was small but worked well as a cat's litter room. The space beside the washing machine on the floor was perfectly suited for the kitty litter box that Daniel had purchased, and a little extra space for the cat to move around.

If only things had worked out differently.

Nora dropped to her knees and opened the pet carrier, her hands shaking as she shoved Blanco inside. He went in too easily, without the slightest resistance, no struggling, just that damn purring as she locked the metal grate behind him. She wasn't going to leave him in the carrier all night, even after all that had happened, but she wanted to see him behind bars, see him contained. She pressed on the latch and twisted it a little to test it. Once, twice, three times. It was secure, yet she still doubted that it could hold him inside for even a single night. Somehow, she knew he would get out.

"What are you doing?" Daniel asked.

She stared at Blanco through the bars of the carrier door. "I don't trust him."

He let out a little nervous laugh. "What are you talking about? You think he's going to break his way out of that thing?"

Yes, that's exactly what I'm saying. But she couldn't say it. "Of course not."

"Then why put him in the carrier?"

"I suppose I'm punishing him," she said. "Solitary confinement."

"He'll need to get to his litter box."

"I'll open the door," she said. "Don't worry." She looked into Blanco's eyes and whispered, "I'll take you back tomorrow. You don't belong here."

Blanco blinked at her but sat motionless in his carrier as if it didn't bother him in the slightest.

Nora took a deep breath, then unlocked the carrier again and stood. She followed Daniel out of the room, switching off the light before closing the laundry door quickly behind her on the way out. She locked it, something she'd never done before. The little notch in the doorknob would provide a way to unlock it in the morning.

"Was that necessary?" Daniel asked.

"To put him in the carrier?" she asked. She nodded. "Necessary for me."

"You really don't like him, huh?"

Nora shook her head. "What's there to like?" She stepped past Daniel, then headed toward the bedroom, grabbing her pillows and blankets from the bed. She ripped them off and dragged everything down the hallway toward the laundry room.

Daniel frowned. "Nora?"

She avoided his gaze until she'd gotten to the front of the laundry room door and dropped everything in a pile in front of it. He was watching her. Kneeling down, she arranged the pillows like a makeshift barrier against the door.

He knelt down beside her. "Nora, what are you doing?"

She arranged the pillows and blankets, preparing for the long night ahead. "I just need to be here tonight."

Daniel watched her for a long moment. "It was a lot of stress, what just happened now. You're grieving and scared. I get it, but—"

"I need to be here," she repeated.

Daniel glanced around, back down the hallway toward Lucy's room. She wouldn't have blamed him if he'd gone back to their bedroom to sleep in their own bed, or argued with her, telling her she was being irrational or paranoid. She wouldn't have blamed him at all. Those reactions made sense. But instead, he sighed and seemed to surrender while moving in beside her on the blankets.

"Then I'm staying too," he said.

His eyes drooped as he lay down beside her, and neither of them spoke. The house settled into an eerie silence over the next hour. No cries from Lucy, no complaints from Daniel. Only the faint hum of the refrigerator downstairs and the distinct ticking of the hallway clock broke the stillness.

When his breathing slowed into a deep, rhythmic snore, she sat up and pressed her back against the door. The dim light coming from the kitchen barely reached her, but it was enough to keep an eye out for anything unusual, enough to catch the first sign of something *wrong*.

She could hear Blanco's soft, muffled purr through the door, and she squeezed her eyes shut.

You'll never get near Lucy again. I'll stay awake all night if I have to.

Blanco let out a series of strange noises. *Laughter?* He was mocking her.

She would need to tell Daniel the truth sooner rather than later. He should know what had happened, even if she didn't fully understand it herself. But for now, she would stay right there with her eyes wide open—the only thing standing between her family and whatever evil lurked just inches behind her.

❧ 29 ❧

At 2 a.m., Nora still lay in the same spot with Daniel next to her. His breathing was slow, and she still sat with her back against the laundry room door, a blanket draped over her legs. It was impossible to sleep now, with Blanco only feet away. She couldn't take the chance of leaving the door, even for a moment.

What was she so afraid of? That the cat would somehow figure out a way to open it, unlock it from inside? No, that was crazy... right? But Lucy might have tried to sneak out of her bedroom and unlock it for him, hearing him meowing from the other side, calling to her in the stillness of the night. She couldn't have resisted his calls of distress.

Her precious little heart.

But he wasn't meowing anymore or making any kind of sound within the darkness. There was no sign that the cat was even still in there. Maybe that was part of its plan—to see how much silence she could endure until she broke down and opened the door to check on him. And then, when she opened the door, he would run off to be at Lucy's side, jump into her arms, and...

And what?

She shivered.

She could imagine a hundred different scenarios, none of them ending in a good way. No fairy tale endings tonight.

A noise finally came from behind her, somewhere deep inside the laundry room—a thump. Her body tensed and her ears perked as she focused on the space behind the door. Something was shifting inside the room, scraping against the wall higher up, about eye level. Turning her head slowly, she followed the sounds until something skittered along the inside of the laundry room wall.

She pictured the cat in her mind. The noises weren't *natural*. Her imagination painted a grim scene: the cat digging its claws into the sheetrock, clinging to the side of the wall, testing every corner for weaknesses to escape from its tiny cell. He wasn't just pacing the room like a nervous cat waiting for its owner to return. No, he'd climbed up somewhere high to find a way out.

She didn't move, didn't breathe. The noises grew louder, and there was a small shuffle of paws shifting across the wooden shelves.

He'd jumped up to where she'd put her laundry soap and fabric softener supplies.

Not surprising that he'd gotten up there. It wasn't such a stretch to believe a cat had climbed up there—just jump up onto the washer and dryer, then a short leap onto the shelf. She followed the sounds in her mind until a thud and a sharp metallic clang filled the silence, followed by the unmistakable rattle of an air vent.

Her stomach dropped. The air vent. Daniel had done some repairs in there a few days earlier. He'd removed the panel, but hadn't he sealed it up when he'd finished? Blanco might exploit the opening, going inside and maybe getting several feet before it would either drop off or rise to the ceiling.

Where did that vent go?

She tried to picture the layout in her mind. The furnace was near the garage, but the ductwork sprawled in every direction. She imagined Blanco scurrying through the maze of ducts, following it from room to room... over to Lucy's room.

A chill swept through her as she tried to remember for certain if Daniel had sealed it back up again or if he had left it open. Even if he hadn't finished the repair, was it even possible for a cat to climb up high enough inside to make its way around safely? Wouldn't it get lost or trapped along the way?

Not this cat.

Another sharp crack jarred her senses, scraping against something like wood until it stopped suddenly. Silence returned a moment later, and her pulse pounded in her ears. She swallowed and shifted her position with her back against the door, pressing her ear against it to better listen to the sounds coming from inside. Cupping one hand around her ear, she pressed it against the door.

Blanco had stopped moving.

The silence lasted for what seemed like an hour as she tried to pick up any signs that the cat was still in the room. Had he gotten out another way? Crawled through a hole behind the washer and dryer, pushing his way through the insulation and around the framing toward Lucy's room with a tenacity in his empty eyes?

It was clear he intended to harm Lucy at the first chance he got. It was only a matter of time if he were allowed to have his way.

But... why?

A moment later, something pushed against the door, pressing into Nora's back—something unlike the change in air pressure and definitely not her imagination.

Blanco was right behind her.

Turning back toward the door, it shifted slightly. Barely perceptible, but it was there. Had the cat made his way down from the air vent to the door in that time, sensing that she was listening on the other side? Something scratched slowly against the other side of the door, its claws digging into the wood and dragging across the space just behind her neck.

She leaned forward. The scratching noises dropped to the floor, and a single white paw flitted out from under the door. She shuddered. It poked out again, and its tiny claws flexed once like a stretch as if daring her to play along.

At the same time, a low, soft whisper came through the sliver of space beneath the door. "She's such a sweet girl, Nora."

Nora froze.

The voice hadn't come from a human or animal but something low and guttural—a twisted, scratchy voice that sent a shiver up her spine. Daniel stirred at the same time, but she hesitated to wake him up. She wanted to scream or cry or do something, but she couldn't move. The voice seemed to come from inches behind her, like someone had pressed their face against the wood.

It started humming a little song. Lucy's favorite song. The same one her daughter had sung to Blanco the previous night, except now it held a mocking tone, with amusement laced into every syllable.

"Daddy burned the bad away,
  But still it comes to play."

Nora opened her mouth to scream but gasped in a breath instead. Blanco slid his paw under the door again, and she lurched away when it slid toward her.

He couldn't get out, so what did she think he might do? Reach through that small space and slash her throat?

"I love Lucy," the voice said. "I love her to death, don't you know that?"

Nora lunged forward and slammed both hands against the door. Daniel stirred again, and there was a pause in his snoring, but he didn't wake up. She wanted to open the door. Run inside, grab Blanco, and throw him out into the cold again, just to get rid of him before Lucy ever had the chance to speak out against it.

But he'd return, wouldn't he? Blanco had already proven that. He would make his way back inside, and there was no getting rid of him in any simple way. He would make his way back to Lucy's window and tug on her heartstrings again, and there was nothing Nora could do about it. The game was rigged. She couldn't win.

A mix of fury and fear twisted inside her chest, but she forced herself to speak. "Stay away from her," she said in a low growl.

A soft thump came from inside, like Blanco throwing himself against the door. Was he trying to break through? Then she heard his footsteps near the far side of the room. He was scurrying from one side to the other as if working himself into a frenzy.

"I'll never let you get near her again," Nora said.

The room went silent again. After several minutes, she even started to believe the nightmare had passed. But the whisper returned a short time later through the bottom of the door, this time a little louder, a little lower, now a man's voice. "I'll always be… right… here," he said. Then a final thump against the door before silence.

She wanted to scream, pound her fists against the door, but she held back to spare Daniel and Lucy from sharing her nightmare.

Shut up, shut up, shut up! Damn you!

It took a long time before her heartbeat slowed again until the only sound coming from the other side of the door was the steady rumble of purring.

Daniel stirred against her and shifted onto his side. He could sleep through anything, it seemed, but it was better that she handle it alone. She would do what she needed to do first thing in the morning. Get rid of Blanco. She would do it, no matter how much Lucy cried or pleaded. No matter what any of them had to say, she would do it because she had to.

"As soon as the sun rises," she said to herself, like a prayer.

"Sweet dreams," came the voice from the other side of the door.

$$\text{❧ } 30 \text{ ☙}$$

The next morning, Nora cautiously opened the door to the laundry room. Blanco was inside sitting next to his carrier. His gaze locked onto her.

Closing the door behind her, she got down on her knees in front of the cat and spoke directly into his face. "I don't know what you were planning to do last night, but you'll never get close to Lucy ever again."

His expression didn't change, although his eyes narrowed just a bit.

Glancing around the laundry room, everything was the same. Nothing was broken. No holes in the wall, nothing torn apart, and no signs that he'd tried to escape, except for a line of claw marks against the back of the door. Whatever he'd tried to do last night, he'd failed, and for just a brief moment, a wave of relief passed through her.

Had she overreacted?

Someone knocked on the door, and she shuddered. Lucy's small voice came from the other side. "Can I come in?"

She gave Blanco a cold stare—

I'm watching you.

—then opened the door just far enough for Lucy to slip inside, closing it immediately behind her.

Nora had already told her daughter they wouldn't be keeping the cat, and Lucy had cried, as expected, pleading with her to change her mind. She hadn't backed down. It was too late for that. Blanco had to go. Daniel had backed her up, but he'd avoided her gaze all morning, no doubt overwhelmed by the situation too.

On top of everything, they had also sat Lucy down and told her that her grandfather had died. They had all cried together over that as well, and it was hard to tell which of the two pieces of news Lucy was more upset about. Daniel had sat on the opposite side of Lucy, and they had embraced each other, although Lucy had folded forward in tears, asking all the usual questions any child might ask about the death of a loved one.

In the end, it was clear: the news had devastated Lucy, and it would take her some time to process what was certainly one of the worst days of her life.

After their talk with Lucy, Daniel had pulled Nora aside, suggesting they keep Blanco a little longer just so the combined trauma didn't push Lucy over the edge. But the truth was clear in his eyes. He was afraid that all the trauma might push *her* over the edge.

"I've made up my mind," she said.

He nodded and kept quiet throughout breakfast. Lucy picked at her cereal, chewing one piece at a time with a heavy frown. She glanced toward the laundry room every few seconds as if she expected Blanco to run out and greet her at any moment. More tears flowed down her cheeks, and her sniffles tugged at Nora's heart, but there was nothing she could do. Nothing any of them could do.

It was for the best.

As Nora prepared to take Lucy to school, she delayed the final task until the last minute. She needed to get Blanco. Stepping into the laundry room again, she found him already sitting inside his carrier as if he understood exactly what was going to happen to him. He didn't seem to care at all. She could take him back, lock him outside, or do anything she wanted to with him, and it wouldn't make a bit of difference.

Heading downstairs, she stopped at the front entrance with the carrier and set it by the door. Lucy ran over, finally blurting out all the pent-up emotions she must have held back at the kitchen table. "You can't take him," she shouted in a high, frantic voice. "You can't do this!"

"Lucy—"

"He's part of our family now. He's my brother. You promised me that I would get a pet someday."

"And we will," she said, "someday."

Lucy touched his carrier. "But we have one *now*. That's why he came home last night after you lost him, because he belongs here. He knows this is his home!"

Nora bent down to face her daughter. "Sweetheart, we'll get you a pet one of these days, and I know you've grown attached to him, but I made a mistake in bringing him here. It's not going to work out."

Lucy shook her head and backed away. "Grandpa was right," Lucy said. "You don't tell the truth. You lie about everything."

"Lucy," Daniel said from across the room.

"He did," Lucy raised her voice. "Grandpa said that about Mommy. He said Mommy lies about everything and he was right."

Her daughter's words stung her heart. She could imagine her father saying something just like that, if only to make himself look better in Lucy's eyes. Lately, he'd praised Lucy's curiosity and interest in the family's business—urging her to absorb everything she could of her mother's craft. To him, Lucy was the answer, a fresh solution to old problems. He'd moved on from Nora and Ally to groom Lucy, the next in line to take over the business as soon as she was old enough.

She could have set Lucy straight in the moment, revealed a

taste of the truth, that her father had taught her everything about deception, but she held back. Lucy had been through enough. Better to break Lucy's illusions about her father another day.

"I have lied in the past for my job," she said. "That's going to change."

"You didn't care about Grandpa, or about me, and now you don't care about Blanco. I hate you."

The words hit her like a slap to the face.

Daniel walked over and stood beside Nora. "Lucy, don't ever say something like that again. That's awful."

Nora pushed down the wave of emotional pain rising in her chest. "I do care, and I know this is hard to understand, but I loved my father, and I love you, and we'll get you another pet. A kitten, or a dog, or anything else—a real pet, one that belongs here. But Blanco has to go back to his home."

"This *is* his home," Lucy trembled as she cried. "I don't want another cat. I want Blanco."

Nora wanted to walk out the door with the carrier and never look back. But it was her problem. *She* had made the mistake of taking Blanco home in the first place. Her attempt to reconcile with Gabriel's spirit had failed, and now she saw her mistake of not getting Lucy ready for school before that moment. "It's not possible to keep him," Nora said. "I'm sorry."

Daniel touched her shoulder. "I don't mind taking Lucy to school," he said.

Nora shook her head. "I'll take her. Let's go."

THE DRIVE TO SCHOOL WAS PURE HELL. LUCY CRIED ALL THE way with her face pressed against the glass and never said a word. Usually, taking Lucy to school was the highlight of her morning, a special time for them to talk and laugh about everything fun in life, so full of joy and optimism. Her daughter's infectious laughter always set her in the right mood, a dose of light against the darkness ahead. But now Blanco had come between them, and he was still there, watching her through the carrier's door.

The silence was agonizing, broken only when they finally pulled up at the school. The student safety aides hurried over to the car, ready to welcome Lucy to class as soon as her door opened. But she didn't open it. Instead, she faced Nora with a pained expression. Tears streaked down her cheeks.

"Don't take him away from me, Mommy."

A fresh wave of pain swept through Nora's heart. She clenched the steering wheel and pressed her lips together. She wanted to give in and say, "Yes, sure, absolutely, you can keep him for another day. Please, just stop crying and love me again." But it was wrong. Everything was wrong. It was absolutely impossible that Blanco would ever step foot in their house again.

"We'll talk about it later." Nora stopped the car at the curb. "Hurry, sweetheart, or you'll be late for class."

Lucy shook her head and threw her arms around Blanco's carrier. "I can't leave him, Mommy. Please don't take him. Please."

"Lucy," Nora said, "I said we'll talk about this later. You can get another pet. Anything you want, I promise."

The student safety aide, a girl not much older than Lucy, opened the door and peeked inside. "Hello," she said with a wide smile.

Lucy wiped her nose on her sleeve and trudged out of the car without another word. She didn't look back.

"Have a nice day!" the safety aide said before shutting the door.

The sound of the door snapping shut broke Nora's heart. It had taken all her strength to stand strong, to do the right thing, but separating from Lucy this time crushed her soul. She had failed her daughter, broken her daughter's heart, failed her father, and she broke down crying before even putting the car into drive.

How could she do this to Lucy?

The student safety aides were frantically waving for her to move forward as the other cars lined up behind her. At least none of them were honking at her yet.

Tears blurred her vision, but she stared into the rearview mirror and met Blanco's gaze. "Goddamn you."

A tall woman wearing a safety vest was approaching her car. Nora wiped away her tears and finally pulled the car forward. Only moments after she turned out onto the main street, a soft noise came from the back seat. It wasn't the sound of a cat meowing or growling at her but something almost... human—a laugh.

Staring into the rearview mirror again, Blanco was pressing his face against the bars of the carrier. He was glaring at her.

"Why are you doing this to me? You killed my father. We're even."

Blanco's mouth fell open as if he might laugh again.

"No, you won't." She thrust her foot onto the accelerator and glanced into her rearview mirror. The force threw Blanco to the back of his carrier, pushing his face out of sight. As he scrambled to recover, the voice came again, not a laugh this time but a whisper, words spoken at the edge of her comprehension.

"You can't run from me, Nora."

Her heart pounded. "I should throw you out the window."

The laugh came again. "I dare you."

"I will," she said.

Speeding faster, the reality hit her. This is what he wanted— for her to lose control of the car in a rage, slam the car into a tree or a telephone pole. He wanted to see her bruised and bloody lifeless body lying in the ditch. "You'd like that, wouldn't you?" She slowed the car. "But that's not who I am. I'm going to fix this, make it right. Don't you understand that? I made a promise, and I'm going to keep it despite what you're trying to do to my family."

At the next intersection, she made a sharp right turn and drove as fast as she could toward the place where it all began: Gabriel's house.

❦ 31 ❦

Nora parked in front of Gabriel's house. The front windows seemed to stare down at her, daring her to approach.

Gabriel's neighbor, Father de la Cruz—where she'd adopted Blanco—was home, judging by the lights on through the windows and the car in the driveway. With any luck, she could drop off the carrier with him, apologize, and be on her way within ten minutes. Then, she would never have to come back there again.

She hadn't glanced back at Blanco since leaving the school. He had meowed a few times, but at least the haunting voices had stopped. Shutting off the engine, she sighed and stepped out of the car. The freezing air embraced her as she rushed around to the rear seat door and opened it.

For just a moment, she caught Blanco's gaze. His gaze met hers—pierced her—and a shiver swept through her.

I tried to make things right between us, Gabriel. I really did.

She lifted out the carrier and turned its door away from her. The cat's weight shifted abruptly to the back as if trying to escape the cold.

Walking up the sidewalk to Father Tony's front door, all she could think about was how Lucy had pleaded with her to keep him.

Please don't take him. Please.

She swallowed and whispered to herself, "I'm doing the right thing, even if Gabriel won't play nice."

Stopping in front of the door, she took a deep breath and knocked. It took a full minute before she heard noises coming from inside the house—the sounds of cats meowing and someone closing a door. Only a few moments after that the door creaked open. Father Tony stood blinking at her in jeans and a flannel shirt. He looked surprised until his gaze dropped to the carrier, then back to her face.

"Nora," he said. "Back so soon?"

Nora smiled apologetically. "Sorry, Father, it's not working out."

He looked at the carrier again. "Didn't take to your place, huh?"

She shook her head. "Something like that."

He sighed and pushed the door open a little wider. "No need to apologize. Come in."

She wanted to simply hand him the carrier and then turn away from the nightmare once and for all. She didn't want to discuss anything with him. How could she explain all the things that had gone wrong since her last visit?

Stepping inside his home, he shut the door behind her and gestured toward the kitchen. The sound of cats meowing and scratching wood came from behind a door near the back of the house.

"Sorry for the delay in getting to the door," he said with a wry grin. "Had to round up my cats before they staged another jailbreak. Would you like a coffee? I'm making one for myself."

"No, thank you, Father. I'm on my way to work."

"Hope he didn't cause you any issues."

"Issues?" She held back a sarcastic laugh. "Couldn't ask for a better pet."

"Maybe you're right," he said. "I guess I'll keep him after all."

Father Tony accepted the carrier and placed it on the floor. Unlatching the door, Blanco stepped out cautiously, then scurried away, his tail flittering through the house as if he owned the place. Nora watched him until he disappeared around a corner.

"What made you bring him back?" Father Tony asked, leading her away from the front door. He stopped in the dining room, pulled out one of the chairs from the table, and sat down on the opposite side. A stack of banker boxes sat along one edge of the table, towering over smaller stacks of paper, folders, and some old photos. "Have a seat."

She accepted his invitation and sat, glancing around the house. A crocheted blanket lay draped over the back of a worn sofa, and a crucifix hung on one wall, adorned with tiny palm fronds tucked in behind it. There were bookshelves stuffed with old Bibles and leather-bound books, along with framed photos of what must have been his family or parishioners. The walls were lined with framed religious art. The only one she recognized was a print of the Last Supper.

"My daughter loved Blanco," she said. "But we decided we can't afford another mouth to feed."

He nodded. "Pets can be expensive, no question about that. My cats consume half my income, it seems, but I suppose adding Blanco to the payroll won't kill me. I gave the letter to Gabriel's brother, like you asked."

"Letter?" Nora searched her memory but came up blank.

"The envelope you dropped off last time," Father Tony clarified. "I made sure he got it. He wasn't sure what the money was for."

Then she remembered. The envelope with Gabriel's cash refund. "For... a refund."

Father Tony gave her a strange look, but one of the boxes on the table caught her attention. It was labeled 'Anna.' A pang of unease twisted in her stomach.

She gestured to it. "Something from Gabriel's daughter?"

"Yes... His brother and I carried a few boxes of Anna's things over to my house to sort through. It's a little warmer here in my dining room." He looked at her curiously for a long moment. "How long did you know Gabriel?"

She took a sharp breath, preparing for another lie but stopped herself. The way he was looking at her... like he already knew the truth but was waiting for her to confess. "I didn't," she admitted. "Not really."

He nodded knowingly. "I had a hunch when you stopped by the first time. You didn't seem like someone who knew him very well."

"He was... one of my clients."

Father Tony leaned back in his chair and stared at her for a long moment. "He visited you?"

"He did," she said. "Once. But that was enough. His reading was a disaster. I went to his house to return his money."

"Why is that?"

She caught herself about to lie again and bit her bottom lip. The habit would take time to break, but she wouldn't lie anymore about what happened with Gabriel. Not to herself or anyone. "He caught me cheating."

His eyebrows jumped. "Cheating?"

"I'm a phony," she said. "One of those frauds he railed against in his suicide note. I fed him all the usual lies, like I do to all my clients, and he caught me lying."

"That's unusual."

"How is it unusual?" she asked.

"The honesty," he said. "Of course, I'm familiar with your family's business, the House of Vale psychic establishment. I've even heard of you before, Madame Lenora. Is that correct?"

"Yes."

"Gabriel mentioned your name before he died. He was desperate in his final days to connect with the spirit world, wanting one last chance to speak with his daughter, Anna. I'm deeply troubled to say this, but he did a lot of *experimenting* in his home. He kept quiet about most of it, but I know he went through tons of books on black magic, channeling, séances, and all sorts of occult topics in his final days. He was obsessed with it right to the last moment. You might have been the last medium to speak with him."

Nora swallowed. "I didn't know."

"You can't blame yourself," he said.

Nora's heart ached. "It's hard not to."

"What a tragedy." He shook his head. "His whole life revolved around that girl after his wife died in a car accident. After she died, Gabriel... he was never the same. He talked about Anna endlessly, even after she passed away."

"He wanted me to contact her."

"Yes. He tried everything."

Nora searched his face. "When you say *everything*..."

Father Tony stared at her for a long moment as if trying to decide whether or not to continue. He glanced back toward the living room, stood up, and then gave a little gesture. "Let me show you something."

She followed him to the hallway closet near the living room. He opened the door, dragged out a weathered cardboard box, and opened it between them. Gabriel's name was written in large black letters on the side.

The box was full of items she might display in her parlor—tarnished silver talismans, several melted candles, and hand-written papers covered in strange symbols. Some of them she recognized—a pentagram, an Ankh, and the Satanic cross—but most of them she'd never seen before.

He dug inside the box and pulled out a worn-out book with warped pages and blackened edges. "This one," he said, "I found near the fireplace."

Another item stood out against all the others—something that didn't belong with the others: a faded pink hair ribbon.

"All of this was his?" Nora asked.

Father Tony nodded and watched her reaction. "I told you,

he tried *everything* to contact Anna. Maybe you can tell me what it is. I pulled it out of Gabriel's house shortly after his death. Gabriel's brother hasn't seen it, and I'm sure as hell not going to show him. Better that his brother remember him the way he was *before* Anna passed away. I thought about throwing it in the trash, but I'm inclined to dowse it in holy water and then burn it all in the fire pit out back after the weather clears up. Even storing it here in the closet doesn't sit well with me."

"I... I really tried to help him." Nora squatted down beside the box and reached in to touch one of the talismans, despite the dread building in her stomach. The moment her fingers brushed against it, a wave of dark energy surged through her, and she yanked her hand back. Blanco let out a strange guttural sound at the same time from the next room as if he were somehow connected with the items inside.

Despite the flash of fear, the pink hair ribbon seemed to call to her. She picked it up cautiously. "Did this belong to...?"

"Anna," Father Tony said. "I remember Gabriel had tied Anna's braids with so much love after his wife had died."

She stroked one finger along the silk surface. "Can I borrow this?"

He hesitated but finally gave an uncertain, "Yes. Of course."

"Thank you." Nora stood again with her pulse thumping in her ears. She slipped the ribbon into her pocket and stepped back.

The connection between Gabriel and Blanco was alive and well, and returning the cat to Father Tony would only delay the inevitable. Gabriel had aligned himself with an evil she didn't understand, and the fury in his heart might still burn bright even after Lucy was dead. She would need to go to the source of his pain to stop the madness. Anna.

"I'm not sure anyone could help him in the end," Father Tony said, putting away the box and shutting the closet behind him. "He was a different man after Anna died, a hopeless wreck. I always encouraged him to seek psychological help, but he chose a darker path to find her, and we know where that led him."

"I'm sorry I couldn't help him."

Father Tony shook his head. "Nobody could."

"Can you tell me where Anna was buried?" Nora asked, trying her best to hide the rising tension in her chest.

He looked at her for a moment. "Hillcrest Cemetery just off Lyndale Avenue. Her gravestone is not far from his, in the corner at the back on the left. His grave is still fresh, so you shouldn't have any trouble finding it. Are you planning a visit?"

"Yes. I owe it to him." Nora stepped toward the door. She had to talk with Ally right away about what she'd seen in the box. This was her sister's territory, and it was clear that things were far worse than she'd suspected. "I should go now."

Father Tony nodded, and his gaze turned toward the darkened hallway where Blanco still hadn't returned. "Don't worry about the cat. I'll take good care of him."

She nodded. "I'm sure you will. Thank you for talking to me. Really."

She hurried toward the door and thanked him again before stepping outside into the freezing air. After she was back in her car, she immediately dialed her phone.

Ally answered on the first ring. "Nora?"

"I just spoke with Gabriel's neighbor," Nora said. "I need to meet you at the Hillcrest Cemetery in an hour. Can you do that?"

A pause, then, "Um, what exactly are we doing?"

Nora swallowed. "We need to do another séance."

❧ 32 ❧

An hour later, Nora gazed over the sprawling rows of headstones, each one a silent marker of a life long since gone. A thin layer of snow covered the cemetery grass. Ally was already there, having followed the directions she'd sent her by text, standing near Anna's headstone with a large duffel bag on the ground beside her. Her sister was standing perfectly still with her arms crossed in the chilly late-morning air, with her car parked at the edge of the narrow road.

She walked up to Ally, who had already placed everything around Anna's grave, and put on her bravest face.

"You look like hell," Ally said.

Nora let out a short, humorless laugh. "That bad?"

"After this is over, I suggest taking a long vacation."

"I will," Nora said. "When this is over. But it's not over."

Ally squatted down beside Anna's grave first and lit the incense. Taking the bundle and waving it in the air.

"This has to work," Nora said.

"It should," Ally said. She glanced at the object in Nora's hand. "Is that it?"

Nora held out her palm, revealing the faded pink hair ribbon.

Ally took it and placed it beside the grave, then ran her fingers over the gray headstone's engraving:

They stared at the heart-shaped granite headstone for a long moment. A tiny angel and a Teddy bear were carved into the stone beside the inscription. The images tugged on Nora's heart.

"You know this is reckless and rushed," Ally said.

"I know," Nora whispered.

"And what makes us think we can contact Anna after Gabriel already tried everything?"

"Because I have faith in you."

Ally straightened a bit. "I'll do my best."

"I'm more concerned about accidentally catching Gabriel's attention instead. He wouldn't appreciate us trying to contact his daughter."

"Then why do it?"

"Because I don't have a choice."

"That's not true," Ally said. "It would be better if we waited a day. It would give me some time to research this. We don't want to make things worse."

"How could this make things worse, Ally? Gabriel killed Dad. He's trying to kill Lucy, and probably me too. It's destroying my family. And if I can bring her back, then... if I can give him what he wants, maybe this will end. Maybe he'll stop."

Ally shook her head. "Remember what happened last time at the parlor. We're rushing into this again."

An icy gust of wind swept through the trees, sweeping against Nora's face and neck. She shivered. "We can't wait."

Ally studied her for a moment, then nodded. "Fine, but let's just *try* to do this right. We'll do all the steps by the book, slowly, methodically. We don't want to miss anything."

"Just tell me what to do."

Nora dropped to her knees opposite Ally as her sister reached into her bag and pulled out a chalk circle drawn on black cloth. She placed smooth river stones at each corner above inscribed sigils. Then she pulled out a small bowl of salt, a silver hand mirror, and a brass bell. Grabbing some of the salt, a pinch at a time, she traced the circle with it. Nora watched uneasily as Ally arranged everything with ritualistic precision. "I'm in your hands."

"God help us," Ally said.

Nora shivered again, not from the cold air but from the fear of what might go wrong. Ally was a stark contrast, moving through the items with control and discipline. How could Nora have gotten through life this far without Ally to guide her through all the chaos? She owed so much to Ally, who had stood by her, a loyal sister over the years, and now it seemed she was her only hope for saving her family.

"Nora." Ally gestured toward the center of the circle. "Have a seat."

Nora hesitated but sat on the section of cloth.

As Ally placed the ribbon on Anna's gravestone, she struck a match and lit a single black candle shielded from the wind by a glass case. Opening a thick book, she flipped to a bookmarked page and started reading a long passage in some strange version of English she barely understood.

The wind died instantly, and Nora glanced around. None of the trees were swaying anymore.

"You should call her now," Ally said, holding Nora's hands with the candle between them.

"How do I do that?"

"Just say her name and do the same thing you did at the parlor. But this time I'll make sure to…"

"How is this any different from what we did with the customers?"

Ally nodded slowly. "Your intention. No money involved. No deception. No mask. And I brought out the real stuff, not the plastic toys you have in your parlor, but the real thing."

"Anna," Nora said in a steady tone. "I'm reaching out to you with all the love and respect I should have shown your father before. If you can hear me, please come forward."

They waited, peeking through half-open eyes. The candle flame flickered, but nothing else happened.

She continued, "Anna, I need to speak with you about your father, Gabriel. He misses you a lot, and I need to speak with you. Please join us in this space. Please."

Ally read the words from the book again, more insistent this time, ringing the bell in a rhythmic chime that echoed through the silent graveyard. Still, nothing.

Nora swallowed. This *had* to work. If she had truly conjured something in the parlor, then at least a part of her was capable of speaking with the dead. "Anna," Nora said with more force and a little louder. "We need to speak with you. Right now. Your father is waiting for you."

Something moved in the air above them. A flapping sound and then a loud caw as a blackbird swooped down and landed on Anna's headstone. Nora stiffened. She met its glossy black eyes for a moment as it stared back at her full of curiosity and... death? Ally glanced over at it but remained motionless.

Another bird dropped and joined it. Then another. Nora's heart beat faster as she glanced around in panic. Something was coming. She could hear the clatter of something in the distance. She could *feel* it.

"Nora, focus on Anna," Ally said. "Forget the birds."

"Anna," she repeated.

At the same time, a dozen blackbirds descended, their wings flapping through the air like dry paper. They crowded Anna's headstone, the branches, and ground around them. There were too many soulless eyes staring back at her. The temperature, even in that frigid air, seemed to plummet even further.

Nora gasped for breath as a cool wind swept around them, chilling her face and hands, and something like a whisper passed through the air.

"She's not here," it said.

The candle sputtered violently, throwing its flame from side to side as all the blackbirds began to caw as if breaking into a loud conversation. They moved in closer, beating their wings and shrieking like tortured souls. Ally screamed and covered her head as some of the birds came up behind her, only inches from her head, taking short bursts through the air to jump from one spot to the other. Flames erupted from the incense, and within the swirling smoke came something vaguely human in form. It stood between them. Only its face held Gabriel's eyes. He stared at her, his black eyes burning with rage.

"You took her from me," he said, his voice broken, crackling.

The blackbirds lunged at them, covering Nora's face as they raked through the air, their talons scratching over her skin as she struggled to shield her face.

Ally swiped her hands over the circle of salt, closing the door to the spirit world. As she scrambled to stand, she helped Nora to her feet. "We have to go."

Nora stood, her hands numb from the pain of the blackbird's injuries now just starting to set in as her body trembled with fear.

Scooping up their items in the black sheet at once, Nora carried it away.

There was no sign of Anna, only Gabriel's wrath. He'd blocked their communication with his daughter, but how had he found them? It was clear she had failed. Anna had been their only hope, and a sinking feeling filled her chest.

She jumped into the car a moment after Ally had climbed into hers. At least, the car helped to shield her from the birds' piercing cries. No, not cries. Shrieking laughter. They were laughing at her. She gasped for breath as the birds swarmed around her car until her phone rang.

Daniel.

She answered it, but he didn't speak right away.

Finally, he spoke, "Lucy."

❧ 33 ❧

Nora's heart raced all the way home. She couldn't help but imagine the worst scenarios of what might have happened to Lucy, despite Daniel's assurances that Lucy was okay. She pictured Blanco somehow finding his way back into the house, or worse, Lucy falling from the roof while trying to rescue him from the tree again. Panic came in waves as she forced herself to keep her foot off the gas pedal. She tried to push away the invasive fears haunting her mind, reasoning that Daniel would have told her if anything *truly* devastating had happened. They had cut the conversation short. He had only asked her to come home as soon as possible.

"Lucy is alright," he'd said, but he hadn't mentioned anything about taking her to the hospital, or about Blanco, or... the police.

Ally followed closely behind in her own car. Nora had tried to explain to her sister what Daniel had said, although she had only nodded, grabbed her things, and charged out to her car, her words broken and slurred with emotion.

They arrived in the driveway seconds apart. Nora charging out of her car first, rushing up the sidewalk without looking back.

All the way home, she'd clung to the hope that nothing

serious had happened. Her heart sank when she arrived at the front door. The screen door was shredded, the wood around the frame slashed and broken. It looked like an intruder had desperately hacked through the bottom section with a machete. Yet the marks weren't made by a blade—they were gouged with parallel lines, deep scars in the wood too similar to the claw marks Blanco had left on the back of the laundry-room door. Only this time, the lines were larger, deeper.

And... blood.

It was smeared along the steps of their wooden porch, spattered everywhere, leaving trails of a large animal's footprints behind.

Not Blanco.

Not this time.

But the blood wasn't... right. The color was off—not a deep red, but a jet black—and it looked too thick, like a slick black jelly.

Ally came up behind her a moment later. "Oh, my God."

After throwing the door open, Nora's heart sank further, seeing the trail of blood across the floor. She rushed inside. "Daniel?" Her voice cracked. "Daniel, where are you? Lucy?"

The sound of footsteps came from the kitchen, although she followed the trail that led straight upstairs to Lucy's room.

Charging up the stairs, Daniel appeared in the hallway just before she entered her daughter's room. His eyes were bloodshot, and he was talking to someone on his phone. He turned the phone away at an angle. "She's okay," Daniel said. "She's in the bathroom."

"Why isn't she in school?" Nora tried to contain her panic.

"The school called me to pick her up. They said she was having some sort of an episode during a movie in class after they turned off the lights. They think she fell asleep and had a nightmare. I don't know, but when I got there, she was curled up in the nurse's office. She said something was chasing her and swears it wasn't a dream. I just told them she hasn't been sleeping well lately."

"What about... all the blood?"

"It's not *her* blood," he said. "An animal got in."

"What sort of animal?"

"A dog."

He looked at her for a long moment, but she couldn't speak. Her mind flooded with images of a dog attacking her daughter. The smell—she hadn't noticed the smell right away, but now it hit her. The rotten stench was nauseating.

Something hung from Lucy's doorknob—the bronze medal Father Tony had given her in Blanco's "Welcome Bag." It was undisturbed, despite the charred black blood that was smeared all over the front of the door.

Nora's heart raced faster as she pushed ahead and opened Lucy's door.

"Oh, thank God." She let out her breath in a rush of relief.

Whatever had attacked Lucy hadn't gotten inside her bedroom, judging by the lack of blood. Despite that, the room was a mess. Her pink bookshelf had toppled over, and her bed was bare, with her bedsheets in a pile on the floor. Closing the door again, she headed toward the bathroom. The dark blood had gotten smeared across the hallway carpet as if someone had tried to paint the floors with it.

"What sort of dog bleeds... black?" Nora asked.

"It might be something else... or chemical contamination," Daniel said. "The animal ingested something—pesticides, oil runoff. It's obviously a stray—no tags—so God knows what it's been eating out there."

"Lucy?" Nora asked and took a deep breath, tapping her knuckle on the bathroom door before opening it.

"Mommy," she answered in a weak voice. Lucy was there, standing in a towel after having just stepped out of the shower. Her bloody clothes sat strewn across the floor. Her shirt was ripped at the collar and down one arm.

Nora dropped to her knees in front of her daughter and pulled her in close while examining her body for wounds. "Oh, no. Oh, no."

Ally picked up the bloody shirt, turning it over in her hands before dropping it again. "Did it bite you?"

"No, Aunt Ally," Lucy said.

"Nora," Daniel came in behind her. "It didn't get her."

Nora glanced around. "Is it gone? Where did it go?"

"It's dead," Daniel said.

"How do you know?" she asked.

"I killed it," he said in a solemn tone. "It might have had rabies or something by the way it ripped through the front door toward Lucy. It didn't last long after it lost blood."

"It kept chasing me, Mommy, even after I told it to stop."

"I got it in the chest a few times..." Daniel said. "But the damn thing wouldn't go down. It kept dragging itself across the floor—sliding—like something was propping it up. Like a marionette."

"I'm sorry," Lucy said in a small voice.

"What do you have to be sorry for?" Ally kneeled down and squeezed her niece. "It's not your fault."

"Did it hurt you?" Nora asked.

"Only a few scratches," Daniel said. "Nothing serious, thank God. If I hadn't been here... if I hadn't been near the kitchen as it came in..."

"I'm sorry, Mommy. I just wanted to pet him. He was nice to me at first. I never saw a dog crawl like that before. I think Daddy broke his legs."

"I stopped him," Daniel said.

"He tried to get into my room."

A chill swept through her. "Daddy said you had a bad dream in class?"

Lucy frowned. "It wasn't a dream. A man was watching me from the window. The same one who was in my closet."

"She said he smiled at her," Daniel said.

Lucy shivered. "He did."

That broke Nora, and she embraced her daughter for a long moment. "We've got to get you to the hospital."

"She's not injured," Daniel said. "Not physically."

"Daddy protected me."

Lucy's words stung. *Daddy protected me.* Not Mommy. Mommy was off at the graveyard attempting to fix things her own way.

"I grabbed a couple of kitchen knives," he said. "The big ones."

There *were* some light scratches running up Lucy's arm, but nothing serious. She stared into her daughter's eyes. "Sweetheart, not all animals are nice."

Lucy nodded, and her lips trembled as if waiting for Nora to scold her. "I ran when I saw his teeth. He had big teeth. I tried to close the door, but he still got in."

"It's okay," Nora squeezed her daughter closer, then looked around again. "Where is…"

He gave a confused look. "Outside. Didn't you see it when you came in? It collapsed on the porch after dragging itself through the house. Animal control is on its way to pick it up, run some tests."

Her heart beat faster. "I didn't see anything out there except blood."

"I locked myself in the bathroom," Lucy whispered. "It scratched at the door until Daddy scared it away. It laughed at me, Mommy. It laughed."

Nora burst into tears, squeezing her daughter again, but Lucy didn't return the embrace, probably fearing she would now get in trouble for all the damage and all the blood.

"You didn't do anything wrong," Nora said.

Daniel glanced in the direction of the front door. "I need to check on something."

"Yes," Nora said. "We'll be right here."

Daniel stared at her with a bit of uncertainty and fear and then hurried out of the room.

"While you get her dressed," Ally said, stepping back with a sympathetic smile. "I'll help Daniel clean up the floors."

Her daughter shivered, and Nora squeezed her tighter. "Tomorrow," she said to Ally, "I'm going to ask Father Tony for his help—beg for it, if that's what it takes."

"Do you want me to meet you there?" Ally asked.

Nora met her sister's gaze and nodded.

"I'll cancel the rest of our appointments," Ally said.

"Thank you."

Daniel came back a minute later, his eyes wide and his lips pressed tightly together like he did sometimes in the peak of an argument. But this was something different. He was... panicked. Even before he spoke, she knew what he would say.

"The dog," he said. "Like you said... It's gone."

34

Right after sundown, Nora picked up Ally at the parlor before continuing to Gabriel's house. Her sister brought a backpack with her and placed it at her feet on the floor of the passenger seat. The black handle of a pistol poked from one of the pockets.

"What's that for?" Nora gestured to it.

"Just in case," Ally replied.

"In case... what?"

"... we see any dogs. Dad always warned us not to bring a knife to a gunfight."

Nora didn't argue after what had happened to Lucy. Whether or not Gabriel had used occult forces to keep his three dogs tethered to this world with him like Father Tony had said, it was better to prepare for the worst.

"I canceled all the appointments just like you asked," Ally said.

"What did you tell them?" Nora asked.

"I said we had a death in the family."

Nora swallowed. "Did you also tell them we might not ever open again?"

"No," Ally said. "Because we *will* get through this."

They were quiet for the rest of the drive. But instead of stopping in front of Gabriel's house, she parked at the one a little further down. The neighbor, Father Tony, had his lights on.

"What if he says no?" Ally asked.

They both knew they didn't have a backup plan. If Father Tony refused to hand over the key to Gabriel's house, the only other option was to break in and risk getting arrested for trespassing.

"I don't want to think about it," Nora said.

She switched off the car, and they raced to his porch, the silent chill of winter flooding in around them. Nora knocked and waited a while. The sound of footsteps came from inside.

When the door opened, Father Tony stood in the doorway wearing an untucked flannel shirt and blue jeans. He squinted at them with tired eyes within the dim porch light until a wide smile spread across his face.

"Miss Nora." He looked at each of them. "And Miss Ally. I figured I might see you again soon."

His reaction caught Nora off guard. "You did?" she asked. "Why is that?"

He glanced toward Gabriel's house. "There's been a lot of activity lately."

She followed his gaze. "That's why I stopped by."

A soft meowing came from behind Father Tony. A moment later, a tabby cat forced its way through his legs and sat at Nora's feet, brushing its tail against her leg.

Father Tony sighed. "They get out sometimes... if I don't close the basement door all the way. She likes to think she's part of the welcoming committee." He opened the door wider while stepping aside, nudging the cat gently out of the way with his foot. "Sorry about that. Please come inside."

They stepped into the entryway, and he closed the door behind them. The cat stayed close as they moved inside. Beside an old mudroom bench sat a line of snow boots, an umbrella, and a shotgun.

Father Tony followed her gaze. "Just in case."

After removing their jackets, he led them toward the kitchen, and the smell of cats caught her attention. A moment later, two of Father Tony's cats rushed out to greet them, circling Nora's ankles, then rushing off to the living room. Blanco had to be there somewhere, maybe watching her from a darkened corner, listening, maybe even aware of what they were planning to do. But his presence wouldn't stop them.

"What do you mean there's been a lot of activity lately?" Ally asked him while holding her backpack to her chest like a shield.

He sniffed. "I was debating whether or not to call you. It's hard to explain. I usually don't go in there after the sun goes down. Actually, never." He turned back to them with a solemn expression. "Things come and go from that place. Maybe it's just my imagination—" He gave a tight grin. "Ah, we both know that's a cheap excuse. The truth is more complicated, isn't it? Gabriel got himself into some nasty business over there in his final days." He gestured to the boxes stacked on the kitchen table. "Why do you think I don't sort through Gabriel's things over there? These boxes aren't light, and I'm old. It's a lot of work to carry them over here, but... it's a lot less... disturbing to work here. Not as efficient, but I need to maintain my sanity, don't I?"

Nora nodded. "We need to go in there," she said softly. "Tonight."

Father Tony's face twitched. "I was hoping you'd say that. God knows, someone needs to go in there and clean it out. But I'm afraid of what you'll find at this time of the day. Better if you wait until the morning... when there's more light."

"We don't have time." Ally squeezed her backpack.

Father Tony nodded. "You'll see a lot of shadows around this time. And noises—I sometimes hear dogs barking in the middle of the night, see their shadows running through the backyard. They don't get around like normal—they slide."

"Like marionettes."

His eyes widened a bit. "Yes. You've seen them too?"

"My husband did, and my daughter," Nora said. "One of them attacked Lucy earlier today on her way home from school. It got into our house."

He gave a pained expression. "Is she...?"

Nora nodded. "Nobody was hurt."

"Thank God."

"The medal you put in Blanco's supply bag... What was it?"

"The St. Benedict medal? For your protection. Just in case."

"Lucy hung it outside her bedroom door," Nora said. "Maybe she thought it looked nice or Blanco might need it, but I think... it worked."

"For now," he said. "I've tried to contain the evil, but what Gabriel opened... A person will sometimes give up everything for the ones they love, even their own soul. Gabriel tethered himself and his dogs—his *children*—to this world through his sacrifice to a demon named Moloch. This is dangerous and not to be taken lightly. He may never emerge from his grief, I'm afraid."

"Anna's death must have broken his heart," Nora said. "And that grief... he's trapped now within that grief. He can't hear Anna calling for him or see her."

"He will, most likely in time, but don't underestimate the depth of his torment and rage. He embraced the darkness to reach his daughter and fell victim to those lies. You should avoid trying to confront him any further. He's trapped in a hell of his own making."

"I think he's trying to kill me," she said, "and my daughter."

"That may be true."

"We can't just walk away from this," Nora said. "We have to face him."

"What are you planning to do?" he asked, glancing at Ally's backpack. "If he's trying to kill you, it's better to let me handle this."

"We tried to contact Anna before at her gravesite," Nora said, "but Gabriel interfered. We want to try again in his house."

Ally spoke up. "We think we can lead Gabriel to her. Once they reunite..."

"Be careful," he said. "You don't understand what you're dealing with."

Nora reached into her pocket and pulled out Anna's pink ribbon and clenched it between her fingers again. The texture soothed her mind for a moment, reminding her of Lucy's childhood innocence. "I'll use this."

"The ribbon?" he asked.

"We've been doing it all wrong. It's not just the ribbon. If we want to lure Gabriel out of his grief then we need to bring her home first. Her room is the anchor. You mentioned before that Gabriel had tied Anna's braids with love after his wife had died. He would certainly remember that special moment, having cherished it long after she was gone. If there's any way to bring Anna out of the spirit world, this is it."

Father Tony stared at it for a long moment. "You think that will work?"

"You don't?" she asked.

He was silent.

Nora swallowed. "And... we have no choice."

"We won't be long," Ally added. "If we start to lose control, we'll get out of there."

"I wouldn't rush anything," he said, stepping over to a kitchen drawer and opening it. He grabbed a small, tarnished brass key. He didn't hand it to her right away. "You know," he said, "when I advised Gabriel to seek professional help for his grief, I never imagined it would come to this."

"None of us did."

He leaned in toward her as if about to tell her a secret, while cupping the key in his hand. "Let me give you a little advice: you'd better shut every door behind you after you go in. They can't open them, but they can slip through if you leave even one a little cracked open. The dogs stay outside in the yard to guard the house. You won't see them until you get close.

They'll see you. As soon as you get inside, shut the door as fast as you can."

"Thank you," Nora said.

"Gabriel killed his dogs in the fireplace. Anna's bedroom is just around the corner and down the hall after you get upstairs. You'll know it's hers." He gestured to Ally's backpack. "You won't need that."

"What?" Ally asked.

"The pistol," he said without judgment. "You can't kill what's already dead."

Ally gestured toward the shotgun near his door. "Then why keep that?"

He followed her gaze and smiled faintly. "Not everything that walks in the dark is a ghost. The shotgun's for the living, not the dead."

Father Tony held out the key, and Nora accepted it, but he didn't let go of it easily.

"Are you sure about this?" he asked.

Nora squeezed the key in her palm. She could only picture Lucy's frightened face, her torn clothes, the blood streaked across the floor. "I've never been surer of anything."

Father Tony gave a little nod. "I can't go with you—I can't run that fast—but I'll be watching out for trouble. If I hear anyone screaming..."

Nora straightened. "You won't need to call anybody," she said. "I'll fix this."

"God help you," he said.

Nora walked beside Ally along the frozen sidewalk toward Gabriel's front door. There was no sign of the dogs or Gabriel, but she believed what Father Tony had said—they were watching her. She could feel their presence, and after what had happened with Lucy and the dog, her heart raced.

Still, they had no other options. This had to be done. It wouldn't take more than thirty or forty minutes, anyway. The whole thing would be over soon, and her life would finally get back on track.

Their footsteps clattered up the cement steps leading to his front door. Neither of them said anything as Nora unlocked the door, opening it easily without creaking.

The sound of rustling, broken branches came from somewhere behind them. A shadowy figure moved, something low to the ground and inching forward. They rushed inside and slammed the door shut before it had a chance to get closer.

A moment later, something thumped against the door, shaking its frame.

Nora gasped. They were in.

But how would they get out?

She pushed the thought away and glanced around.

Ally switched on a light. A glass chandelier hung directly above them, something Nora hadn't noticed on her first visit to the house. It wasn't anything spectacular, just a remnant of the home's historic years, but the teardrop-shaped crystals resembled daggers ready to impale them if they dared to venture beneath it.

The wood floors creaked with every step and echoed through the house. It was freezing—maybe even colder than outside. The massive fireplace loomed over them from across the living room, its gaping black mouth even more menacing in the dim light, and the smell of burnt wood drifted through the air. Nora held her breath until they'd passed it.

Stopping at the bottom of the stairs, Nora stared up into the darkened corridor ahead. They were almost there.

Ally flipped the light switch, but it didn't work. "There's still time to bail."

Nora let out a little laugh and stepped up the stairs first, with Ally following. "I thought you were the brave one here."

"You were born first."

After they reached the top, Nora glanced around. It was darker than expected. Ally tried the light switches again without success. All the window shades were pulled down, yet the dim light from outside—the moon, the streetlights—provided enough illumination for them to see their way around. She was used to working in the dark anyway. She had a sixth sense about moving in that space, in that familiar world. Still, she pulled out her phone and switched it into flashlight mode to light the way. Ally did the same.

She hadn't gone up there during her previous visit, but from what Father Tony had mentioned earlier, Anna's bedroom was at the end of the hallway.

Moving forward slowly across the creaking floors, they paused in front of an open door. A large queen bed sat empty, flanked by two nightstands. This had to be Gabriel's bedroom. The weight of the tragedy tugged at her heart. A sickening energy reverberated through her body like nothing she'd experienced in all her years of performing behind a séance table. This was *real*—as real as the dog that had attacked her daughter—and the pistol stuffed in Ally's backpack comforted her... for a moment until Father Tony's words came back to her.

You can't kill what's already dead.

"What are you thinking?" Ally asked.

"I want to go in there," Nora said.

"What for?"

She had no answer but something welled up inside of her. She wanted to go into the man's bedroom and scream in the place where he'd slept, to disturb his peace, to defend her family, and to protect her daughter from his attacks. How dare he terrorize Lucy, who had nothing to do with Nora's mistake?

Nora shivered.

"Hard to believe it could get any colder in here," Ally whispered, "but it sure feels like it did."

She inched forward and then turned away.

Ally nudged her toward Anna's room. "We don't have much time."

Nora nodded. A door was open at the end of the hallway. Even from that distance, she could see inside Anna's bedroom. The walls were painted pink, and a small dresser confirmed what she already knew: This is where they would set up and finish what they had started.

They hurried forward and entered Anna's room. The scent of flowers lingered in the air—a vase on the dresser was filled with dried flowers, and a small trash can overflowed with more of them on the floor. A twin bed sat untouched against the far wall, the sheets tucked neatly into the corners, and a handful of stuffed animals lay propped up against a pink headboard. A broken dollhouse sat in the corner along with a child's white makeup table and mirror. The design was simple and feminine, with stickers of hearts and smiling cartoon faces stuck along the edges.

Nora shivered. The icy air stung her face. Had it gotten even colder after they'd stepped inside?

One window blind was pulled up, revealing the backyard in shadow below. Nora crept toward it as Ally dropped to her knees beside the old dresser and started arranging the candles on the floor.

"We'll find her here," Ally said.

"I know we will." Nora nodded and glanced out the window. She forced herself not to look down at the backyard where the dogs might meet her gaze. Father Tony's house was in view now. A dark silhouette appeared in one window. She recognized his hunched posture—he was watching, as promised.

But there was something else watching them from another window near the back of Father Tony's house. Another small silhouette stared back at them with eyes that seemed to fade to black, replaced by a bottomless void.

Blanco.

＊ 35 ＊

Ally moved swiftly to create the space for them, throwing out the black blanket with the pre-printed lines on it and the circles and spaces for them to place all the candles in the right position. Everything was laid out. Then she pulled out another object from her backpack—Anna's ribbon—and placed it in the center of the circle. Nora stared at it for a moment, then met Ally's gaze.

"I can't leave here until this is over," she said.

"Then forget everything Dad taught us at the parlor," Ally responded. "Follow my instructions, and we'll get through this alive."

Ally hurried around the blanket, lighting the candles and chanting some text from a book over and over. The words were mesmerizing, the way she chanted them softly.

Nora's gaze stopped at a drawing on the wall. It showed a sun with a crooked smile and two stick figures holding hands. Anna must have created it, judging by its style. It reminded her so much of Lucy's drawings. There was a date at the bottom: June 15th, 2024, written in pencil by an adult. Nora did the math. Lucy would have been the same age.

Nora's heart ached for everything that had happened in that

house. The guilt swelled, but she pushed it away as quickly as it rose. This wasn't a time for feeling sorry for herself. This was her time for action. A time for answers.

Dropping onto the blanket, she sat cross-legged in the place where Ally directed her. Somehow, it was all unfamiliar, despite everything she had trained for as Madame Lenora. This wasn't theater anymore. This was the real thing. And she watched with wide eyes as Ally meticulously created a circle of salt and iron shavings around the edges of the blanket.

"This is stronger than before," Ally said, without looking up. "It'll keep us safe."

Safe from what?

The hellish image of Gabriel's shadowy figure flashed through her mind, and the way he had manipulated her father like a puppet as he squirmed in his recliner, held hostage by some unseen force. Would Ally's extra precautions really hold back Gabriel's demon dogs if they somehow broke through the door to stop them?

A heaviness descended over the room, and a deep chill swept through her chest.

She lifted the ribbon from the center of the circle and held it in her hand for a moment. Just a faded blue strip of fabric, frayed at the edges. Gabriel must have tied Anna's hair every morning with it. The photo she had seen downstairs during her previous visit reminded her of the way he must have smiled at her in the mirror. She laid it down gently in the center of the circle again, and her stomach churned.

Ally glanced over at her as if sensing her unease. "Are you okay?"

Nora didn't answer. The heaviness wasn't coming from her anxiety this time. It was penetrating her blood, her muscles, her bones. "I feel like he's with us here now."

Ally glanced around. "He probably is."

"When will we know? What should I do when the time comes? Should I just—"

Ally held up her hand. "Just follow directions."

Nora nodded. "I'm going to do everything you say exactly, step by step."

"This won't be anything like you've done before, but... keep it authentic." Ally finally sat down opposite Nora, and the candles flickered even in the absence of wind. There was one candle left in the center, and Nora held her breath as Ally struck the match to light it. "You don't need to impress anyone."

Nora met her gaze. "This could spiral out of hand quickly."

"I have faith in you."

"That's what I'm afraid of," Nora said. "If you'd seen the look in his eyes when I saw his ghost in Dad's apartment... The rage..."

"He's not just angry," Ally said. "Remember, he's also consumed by grief. That's how we'll get to him. I believe in you."

Nora nodded and glanced back at the little sun drawing on the wall again as Ally began chanting in a low, rhythmic tone. Nora joined in, repeating the words at the same time. There was a force behind Nora's words, something she'd never experienced before. An energy that might not have been felt anywhere else, as if they were pushing through water, pushing flames through darkness. The house creaked and groaned around them. The window rattled in its frame, and the freezing air became even colder—cold enough for them to see their breath.

The candles dimmed as if some unseen energy were sucking the light out of the room. Something had arrived. A weight dropped again in her chest—not the fear this time or dread, but grief. Someone else's grief, like the crushing moment you realize the person you love is gone and they are never coming back.

The candle flames flickered suddenly and then burst violently tall, and the mirror on the makeup table darkened—not with shadow, but with movement, reflecting something that was standing just behind Nora. She could feel it bristling against the edges of her neck, the back of her ears, her hair, bristling lightly as if static had caught the ends. And it grew stronger. Something was watching her.

"Gabriel," Nora whispered, "we need to speak with you. I know you're here."

The mirror seemed to warp, but she didn't dare move or look around. The window shuddered as if the force of a tornado were behind it. Every candle flickered wildly again but remained lit within the circle. Ally let out a gasp and grasped the protective amulet around her neck.

"The circle's holding," she said. "Keep talking to him."

Before she could say anything else, the makeup table's mirror cracked, its lines spidering across the surface. Its glass fogged over, leaving a small area thicker near the center as if someone were breathing on it from the other side.

A whisper passed through the air, not from around her but from somewhere inside the mirror. It held a sarcastic tone.

"Madame Lenora."

$§$ 36 $§$

Gabriel called out in a mournful tone. "Where is she? Where's my Anna?"

At the same time, something slammed into the window. Nora shuddered. Birds battered against the window, their sharp, violent sounds filling the air. The glass was holding them back, but for how long? The sound was maddening, and the frenzy outside the window escalated louder and louder.

Another noise rose above the others. The clamor of barking dogs. It was coming from somewhere in the yard below the window. The dogs were clawing at the side of the house. The roaring rage shifted from one side to the other. Were they testing all the windows and doors for weaknesses?

Only a moment later, something downstairs shifted. The air pressure changed. The frenzy of guttural snarls and growls had exploded much louder, much clearer. No sound of breaking glass or wood, but still, somehow, they'd gotten in.

Nora glanced at the bedroom door. She had closed it on the way in, but had the latch clicked shut? She started to get up, but Ally gestured for her to stay down.

"We can't break the circle," her sister said.

The house rumbled under the weight of something rushing

up the stairs. Nora clenched her teeth in panic and resolve. They were surrounded. No way out if they failed. The savage growls echoed through the hallway, the stampede heading straight for Anna's bedroom.

They will tear us apart when they get inside.

And then the door exploded under the weight of their bodies.

The door frame cracked, but it held.

But how had they gotten into the house? Father Tony had said they couldn't get past a closed door. Or had someone let them inside?

The deafening chaos swelled around them.

"Madame Lenora," the voice came again.

Then... silence.

The barking and the birds stopped, except for the sound of panting dogs hovering inches behind the door and the flutter of wings behind the window. Something had directed them to move away.

The voice in the mirror spoke, "You're not welcome here."

"We came to end this," Nora said.

The candle flames burst higher and Nora's heart raced. She reached for the ribbon, but it was no longer at the center of the circle. It was rising gently into the air. Nora strained to grab it, but it hovered just out of her reach.

"You took this from her," Gabriel said.

"You left it behind," Nora replied.

"You stole it," he said. "It wasn't enough that you deceived me in my grief. Now you desecrate her bedroom with your lies."

"It's the truth."

The air warped around them, and the walls seemed to shift. Ally screamed something in Latin—a series of words that she repeated over and over in a solemn chant. The room straightened a bit, like she had taken control of the oppressive force, until the mirror on the makeup table exploded. Shards of glass burst into the air, some of them missing their faces by inches.

"You don't deserve to live," he said. "Not you, not your sister, not your family."

The candles all went out at the same time. Her sister tried to light them again, but Nora doubted it was necessary anymore. Gabriel was there with them.

His figure appeared first as a shadow near the makeup table —a wispy haze hanging in the air like the smoke now rising from the extinguished candles. He seemed to manifest out of nothing, shifting like smoky tendrils in a form that more resembled a black cloak than a human body. Within his form, his blackened eyes took shape, and all the gory details became clear.

Not eyes. Empty sockets.

Blackened blood leaked down over his cheeks like tears that had burned their way out. The shredded flesh around the empty sockets screamed of the self-mutilation he'd endured to gouge them out. The knife hadn't just taken his sight. It had taken his humanity.

His mouth hung open, frozen mid-gasp. There was no sound —except for the drips of blood from his face hitting the wood floor.

He didn't walk. He hovered inches above the ground, just outside their summoning circle. Pieces of his form shifted and moved, like a nightmare struggling to remember its shape.

The walls and floor shook again, groaning under the pressure of the animals silently trying to break in to join their master. The birds had succeeded at her parlor, crashing through the plate-glass window, so what was holding them back now? Was Ally's circle so powerful?

An unsettling energy bristled through the air moments before Gabriel's voice exploded in the room. "What did you do to my daughter?"

Nora opened her mouth to answer but closed it again. She wasn't there to argue with him. This wasn't about strength. They had to get Anna with them there in the same room. Somehow, they needed to pull her in, in this moment, to bring them together. It was the only way out.

Ally was chanting something else, a different line of Latin, although it held no meaning to Nora.

"Ally," Nora said, "where is she?"

Ally paused to answer. "I'm working on it."

The temperature dropped even further. Nora turned to face Gabriel directly. She stared into the hollow eyes of a man she once pitied. "Gabriel," she said, "Anna is on her way. You'll see her soon."

"More lies!" Gabriel shouted.

"You're wrong," Nora said. "She's on her way."

Anna's twin bed rose into the air and flew across the room, scattering the girl's stuffed animals across the floor. The bed slammed into the wall behind them and crashed down with a booming thud. Dust rained down from the ceiling a moment later, filling the air with a murky haze. It was only a matter of time before the window shattered and a flood of blackbirds and ravenous dogs came rushing in. She could see the blackbirds watching them through the cracks in the blinds. What were they waiting for?

Gabriel.

He was holding them back.

Nora wanted to cry but instead reached again for the ribbon floating in the air. She jumped for it. Gabriel seemed to freeze at the same time, his burning empty eyes locking on it. Then, like something invisible swept through the room—a delicate wind, warmer than any of them. The ribbon twisted in the air softly. She touched its edges for a moment, felt its torn, frayed edges against her fingertips before something yanked it away. A soft light formed around the ribbon like a cocoon as it hovered in the air.

"I did it!" Ally said at the same time.

A little girl's voice came a moment later. "Daddy?"

❦ 37 ❦

The ribbon dropped to the floor, and the room went still and silent.

Anna's small voice came again. "Daddy?"

A ball of light appeared near the center of the circle, like a tiny spark hanging in the air between them. It rapidly took form until a young girl stepped out of the emptiness. She appeared in a flowing white dress that drifted in an invisible breeze. Her face was soft and luminous, with the corners of her mouth curled slightly upward like a mischievous grin—a characteristic she must have carried in her life. Her shoulder-length black hair shimmered faintly in the dim light.

She turned toward the swirling shadow that was Gabriel and peered fearlessly into his eyes. "Daddy, I'm here."

Gabriel flinched, and his breath cut short.

"Gabriel," Nora whispered. "Anna is calling for you."

He stood motionless, but his horrifying empty gaze was fixed on something beyond her, beyond them all.

"Liar," he said. "You won't fool me again."

Anna spoke again, softly and clearly. "You don't have to be angry anymore, Daddy."

Nora's heart melted at the sound of Anna's words. The girl

stood inches in front of her father, yet they might as well have been miles apart. He seemed not to recognize her.

Gabriel staggered back, and his shadowed form writhed. "She's not here," he growled. "You're trying to trick me again. You're a fraud."

Nora shook her head. "No. She's trying to reach you. You have to listen. Please, Gabriel."

His form solidified a bit, and deep lines of grief appeared across his twisted face. The sorrow had caught him off guard, but the rage was forming again. "You took her from me. Every... single... one of you lied to me."

"No, Gabriel—"

His hand shot forward, a slithering shadow erupting from his palm. It broke through the circle and wrapped around Nora's throat. She screamed, but the smoky form cut it short. She clawed at the form, her mouth gaping, fighting for another breath.

Ally jumped from her seat, slashing her hands through the line of smoke. The form held its shape. She let out a desperate scream. "Gabriel, stop! This isn't her fault."

"You think this is *my* fault then?" The shadows around Nora's throat tightened, and her vision blurred.

"Gabriel," Ally cried. "She's trying to save you."

"I love you, Daddy," Anna's small voice came.

For a moment, Gabriel froze, relaxing his grip on her throat. Nora gasped a ragged breath.

Ally crawled to the edge of the broken circle and fumbled with the sigils, redrawing the lines in cracked charcoal with her eyes full of tears. She chanted another Latin phrase over and over.

Yet Gabriel still didn't let go.

"I can't see her!" he screamed. The candles burst into flames again. "She's not here. Liars!"

"She's right here," Nora said. "In front of you."

His face twisted again. "I'm going to kill you now. And then your family. Because of what you did to me. You did this to yourself."

"Anna, please," Nora begged the darkness. "Keep talking to him."

But the air had changed. The smoky form wrapped around Nora's neck tightened again, her hands reaching toward Nora for help, for protection. Her vision faded again as Ally's wide, tearful eyes refused to blink from across the circle.

Something thudded against the window. The birds had erupted again, and the house trembled. Their cries filled the air. A rising barrage of their silhouettes slammed against the glass. Wings flailing. Beaks stabbing. The incessant rhythm built quickly.

It was clear—in a moment, the glass would shatter and she would die with her sister.

Nora could feel the pulse in her ears, her energy fading like a candle being extinguished. The temperature dropped further. Behind the bedroom door, the dogs started growling again, low at first, then guttural, frantic barks as they clawed against the door, thumping against it over and over.

"Gabriel," Nora said with her last gasp. "Anna is here."

Her words only seemed to anger him further. His attention snapped toward Anna's dresser. It rumbled to life and then flew across the room, crashing into the window and shattering within shards of glass that flew in every direction. Blackbirds flooded in with piercing shrieks like a river of bubbling tar. Their black wings fluttered wildly. Their claws and beaks slashed at everything around them.

Ally screamed and covered her head. "Gabriel, stop!"

He wasn't listening. Turning toward Anna's bed next—her sheets still folded with care, the pillow still holding the shape of her head. He ripped the comforter free, slashing across the mattress with invisible knives. Its wooden frame cracked and groaned beneath an invisible force. It rose into the air and then flew at the door. The wood splintered and broke away as the mattress slammed into it, breaking the door from its frame, and leaving a gaping hole only a little smaller than the dogs. The circle was broken. Nothing would stop them now.

The pit bull pushed its snout through the opening, its hollow black eye sockets scanning the room. Two more dogs joined in, tearing their teeth into the shattered frame, the broken fragments lashing across their skin and fur, tearing away bits of their own ashen flesh in its pursuit to get inside.

Ally reached into her backpack and pulled out the pistol, tears flowing down her cheeks. "I'm sorry. The circle's not going to hold." She aimed it toward the door and waited.

Nora's heart pounded in her chest. She turned to Gabriel, making a wide gesture to grab his attention. "Look at Anna. She's *right there*."

No answer. He was expressionless now, seemingly pleased with himself to watch the violence that was taking place in front of him.

"Gabriel, please," Nora said. "Please…"

And then—BOOM.

The sound shattered the madness like a crack of lightning. It hadn't come from inside the room, not from Ally's pistol, but from the hallway. The blast blew off the lower half of the door and tore into the pit bull's flank at the same time. Black inky blood exploded across the floor, its flesh bursting apart in a cloud of dry rot and ash. It crumpled forward, smoke erupting from one side. Half of it was missing—obliterated—including the occult symbol Gabriel had branded into him.

BOOM.

The second dog, the Doberman pinscher, dropped to the floor just inside the door. The shot ripped across its chest, taking out all four of its legs, leaving a clump of crumbling innards exposed. Blood splattered and oozed from the wounds as it convulsed and twisted to stand again. It turned its face back to Nora and used its jaw to struggle forward a sliver at a time. Even now, it hadn't given up.

The third dog, the German shepherd, charged inside, seemingly undeterred by what had happened to the others.

Ally screamed.

Nora turned to face the smoke-filled hallway. The last section of the door broke away, knocked off the frame by a man in a brown leather coat wielding a shotgun.

Father de la Cruz.

"Get back," he yelled, racking the shotgun. The dog turned back at Father Tony and lunged at him.

BOOM.

Blood sprayed across Nora's face and clothes. She gagged and spat away the chunks that had touched her lips. It tasted like rotten meat and stank of iron and burnt bone.

The dog fell hard, skidding across the floor, its face decimated in the blast. Gone—everything above its neck. Its carcass crumpled to a stop, landing with the occult symbol facing up. Its headless frame still twitched and writhed as the black ooze leaked from its gaping wounds. Somehow, it was still alive.

Father Tony faced them with wide eyes. His expression was full of fear and resolve. Blanco came up behind him and stopped at his feet. The cat seemed to approve.

❧   38   ❦

N ora's ears rang from the shotgun blasts, and the smell of gunpowder filled her nostrils.

Father Tony stepped into the room and lowered his shotgun. His boots crunched over the broken glass and black jelly blood while black feathers drifted in the air like ash. The blackbirds stood their ground along the windowsill and crowded the floor, still fluttering and jostling within an icy breeze that swept in around them. Some birds were perched on what remained of Anna's furniture. All of them held contempt in their black eyes.

When Father Tony saw Gabriel, he stopped, and his mouth dropped open. "Gabriel?"

There was no response. Instead, Gabriel turned his focus to Blanco, who had also stepped into the room beside Father Tony. The cat's head tilted, meeting Gabriel's gaze for a moment before rushing across the debris to sit within Anna's presence, the blood sticking to its paws along the way.

"He can see her," Ally said, following Blanco's path to Anna.

Nora stared at Anna. The girl lifted a hand toward her father. Her green eyes radiated a soft glow. Her bright face held nothing but peace—a stark contrast to her father's rage.

Instead of looking at his daughter, Gabriel turned his gaze to

Father Tony, then to the birds, then to his broken dogs. The dogs still hadn't given up, their growls harsh and low as they struggled to rise. The fragments of their flesh shifted on their own—each tiny piece—and crept toward the larger chunks as if trying to piece itself back together. Gabriel passed over Anna as if he still couldn't see her.

"Daddy," Anna said. "Don't you see me?"

Gabriel took a sharp breath and shuddered before turning his gaze to Nora and Ally. "Is this another trick? I'll drag you both with me to hell for your deception."

"I'm here, Daddy," Anna said. "I'm right here."

Gabriel's face twisted as if a jolt of pain had swept through him. His face turned pale as he winced. "No. You won't fool me again."

"Look at me," Anna said a little louder.

"It's true, Gabriel," Nora said. "Your daughter is standing right in front of you now. Don't you see her?"

The lines on his face deepened with his growing frustration. "You're lying."

"We're not lying." Ally pointed to Anna. "Why don't you see her?"

Gabriel stared into the space above Blanco and then staggered back as if something had struck him. "No," he whispered. "No, this isn't real."

"It *is* real," Nora said.

"Please, Daddy." Anna's eyes filled with tears as she stretched out both hands toward him. "Don't be mad anymore."

Confusion flashed across his face, and his posture slumped under an invisible weight.

Anna cried louder, tears flowing down her cheeks. "I love you, Daddy."

The air shifted, and his eyes widened. "You're... here," he said.

"Yes." Anna's face brightened as she met his gaze. "I'm right here."

His eyes radiated clarity for the first time. "Is it really you?"

"I came to bring you back," she said.

He nodded. "Yes, yes. I tried to bring you back, too. I thought if I could just find the right words or the right ritual, I could—"

"You couldn't see me then, Daddy. Sometimes I even stood right in front of you. You called out my name, and I called back, but you didn't answer me."

Gabriel dropped to one knee in front of her. "Anna," he said, "I'm so sorry. I only wanted to stop you from... dying. How could I live without you? I tried everything to fix you—to save you."

"I didn't need to be saved. It was just my time."

"And then after you were gone... I needed to see you one last time. Why couldn't I see you then?"

Anna didn't answer, so Nora stepped in. "Because we lied to you," Nora said with a shiver. "You're right, Gabriel, and this is all for you—to make things right."

Gabriel turned to Nora and Ally with a piercing gaze, but the intensity faded a moment later. He bowed his head and stared down at the occult symbol branded into the side of his chest. "I've made a mess of things. I'm not sure he'll let me go."

"Moloch," Ally said.

"It's too late for me," he said.

Anna reached out and took his hand. "It's not too late," she said. "Just keep your eyes on me. It's easy."

With Anna gently leading him, he stepped forward, inching through the edge of the circle that surrounded Nora and Ally. The moment his hand crossed the threshold, flames burst from his charcoal flesh. He didn't scream but instead seemed to surrender to the transformation as the layers of scorched skin peeled away like snakeskin. The material curled and crumbled, dropping to the floor in trails of smoke.

When the symbol on Gabriel's chest passed through the circle, the blackbirds erupted in a chorus of shrieks. Some of them broke into flight out the window, while others backed away. One of them let out a frenzied scream that pierced the air, and Nora covered her ears while Ally watched wide-eyed, still gripping her pistol.

Gabriel's raging green eyes softened as a bright form emerged within his shadow body—a spirit body, like a moth escaping from a cocoon—a ghost of light, matching Anna's radiance. He continued through the circle toward his daughter—his gaze locked on her face—following her to the other side, leaving behind every part of his former shell, just a pile of ashes and blackened matter.

The room trembled softly as a vibrant energy permeated the air and everything around them. The space warmed. "I can see you now, clearly," Gabriel said, facing Anna on the other side. "I never thought I would see you again."

Anna pulled him a little further away from the circle, and Blanco paced at their feet.

"I missed you," Gabriel whispered to Anna.

"Let's go," she said.

They faded together into the quiet stillness and disappeared.

$$\maltese \quad 39 \quad \maltese$$

The blackbirds broke into flight and scrambled toward the window, bursting into the evening air. Their wings cracked against the window frame and sliced against what remained of the glass around the edges. More shards broke loose and hit the floor on their way out. The chaos of their exit filled the room as feathers flew in every direction, and their shrieks drowned out the moment of peace that had passed between Gabriel and Anna.

As the room fell silent again, the chunks of dog flesh finally stopped moving. What remained of their bodies seemed to melt before their eyes. Thick black smoke rose from the fragments as if a hellish furnace was consuming each piece from the inside out. The trail of blood, once thick and glistening, hardened into black, crusted streaks. All traces of the dogs were reduced to the memory of violence and soot.

A moment later, the sound of police sirens came from somewhere in the distance.

"You should both leave now." Father Tony stepped forward, placing the shotgun on the floor. "There's no need to involve you in any of this. The officers know me from when I found Gabriel's body. I can handle their questions just fine. My presence here won't surprise them."

Ally gestured to the shotgun. "I thought you said guns wouldn't help?"

"I said it wouldn't kill them," he answered. "I wasn't sure mine would do much either, but... it bought us enough time. And... I blessed the shells. I've never blessed a shotgun shell before. Never thought to."

Nora looked down at the occult symbol they had drawn on the floor. "How are you going to explain all of this?"

"Vandals," Father Tony said. "They won't question it—especially not a priest. Not after all the misfortune that happened here. I'll say vandals broke in, almost set the place on fire, and I chased them away."

"With a shotgun?"

Father Tony grinned. "The police know me. If you'd seen the carnage Gabriel left behind on the way out last time..." He looked toward the remains of the dogs. The black mounds of ash and debris looked nothing like the beasts that had terrorized them only minutes earlier. "Those animals were not natural in any sense of the word. Now... go."

Nora and Ally scrambled to gather up their items and rushed toward the door. Nora glanced back one last time at Blanco before leaving. "What's going to happen to him?"

Father Tony glanced down at Blanco. "He can stay with me." He gave her a curious look. "What are you thinking?"

She shrugged. She looked into Blanco's eyes. The cat's empty sockets were filled now with the most beautiful copper eyes she'd ever seen. "Can I still change my mind?"

"About what?" Father Tony asked.

She gestured to Blanco. "Can I take him back?"

Without saying another word, Blanco stepped over to Nora as if he had understood her request. He stood at her feet and glanced up at her, his white fur blackened with feathers, ash, and crusted blood.

Nora scooped him up.

"Looks like Blanco already made the decision," Father Tony said. "He's yours."

"Lucy will be happy."

"We'll talk later," Father Tony said.

"I promise," Nora responded, hurrying out the door. She kicked through the black matter left behind by the dogs. The symbol of Moloch was still faintly visible within some of the shapes left behind, although they more closely resembled mole-hills than anything that had been alive.

After rushing out the front door, police car lights beamed through the trees a couple of blocks down the street. Jumping into their car, Nora drove away even before she'd put on her seatbelt. The police cars arrived moments later in her rearview mirror, parking in the same spot where she'd just left.

Father Tony would have a hard time explaining the shotgun blasts, the black debris, and all the damage in Anna's bedroom, despite his explanation of vandals. Nora hoped the old man's confidence and explanation were enough to satisfy them.

On the way home, Ally held Blanco in her arms, making baby talk to the cat the entire trip.

"We'll take good care of you," Ally said. "Don't you worry about a thing. The awful nightmare is over—for everyone—and Lucy will be *so* happy to see you again."

Nora glanced over at her sister. "I never thought I'd dare to take him back home again, not after everything that happened."

"I think you probably misunderstood him this whole time," she said. "I never saw anything wrong with him."

"Well, *something* got into him," Nora said. "But he's different now. I can see it in his eyes."

"You *do* have some psychic abilities," Ally said. "Or you wouldn't recognize it in others."

Nora furrowed her brow. "I'm not so sure about that, Ally Cat."

"It's in our genes," Ally said. "Nothing to be ashamed of. Maybe you don't need to step away from séances."

Nora shook her head. "Those days are over. Dad pressured me to perform like a circus monkey, and I'll never go back to being a fake medium again."

"Not talking about anything fake," Ally said. "We've seen what we can do. We can do it the right way."

Nora considered it for a moment. "What's the right way? You seem to know a hell of a lot more than I do about all this stuff. Why don't you take the steering wheel for a while? I'll sit in the back seat and let you decide where the business goes from now on. How does that sound?"

"Love it," Ally said, lifting Blanco into the air, making small kissing noises near his face. "It's a chance for us to set things straight."

Nora nodded once.

That was it. They had made a decision, and it felt good.

"No more theatrics for the cash," Ally said. "We'll keep it real."

"Agreed." A sense of relief washed over Nora. It was time to right some of the wrong she'd done to her clients.

Ally squeezed Blanco against her chest, and he purred loudly.

A 40 A

The parlor was empty when Nora stepped inside that morning. No voices, no whispers, no creaking floors or rushing to research the next client. The anxiety of preparing for the day's fraud was gone. This was her future—not her father's— and she embraced it.

Nora closed the door behind her and stood in the doorway with her hands stuffed into her coat pockets. Her boots were wet from trudging through the slushy snow on her way from her car to the front door. The world hadn't stopped turning. She would need to make a living somehow, and it seemed Ally's transformation of their parlor had worked. She had booked a dozen new clients in the first week alone, with more scheduled for the following week.

Ally had stripped away all the theatrical props in the parlor— all the hidden bells, electronics, trick candles, and phony ecto- plasm—and replaced everything with her own touch of authen- ticity. She chose things with historical occult value, reminiscent of old Victorian spiritualism, Jewish mysticism, and tarot cards. These were items that she felt could honestly express their new direction.

She had also placed new artwork on the walls, added some

hanging lanterns, and removed the theatrical velvet chairs in the front room. Instead, she focused on creating a place of research and experience, where their clients could talk about everything paranormal and share their supernatural experiences without fear of being mocked.

Ally had done a great job with the new branding as well, shedding the gothic decor their parents had pushed for its dramatic impact. Her sister had left one old parlor item intact and untouched—their original séance table, which had been passed down through their family. It was a nod to their heritage and a reminder of their commitment to moving forward without erasing the past completely.

They would still use the séance room, but Ally removed the effects. She'd brought in more of her books, taking down the velvet curtains and replacing them with bookshelves that she soon filled with delight. She also changed the social media marketing to emphasize authenticity with lines like "Come only if you're ready for the truth." and "We believe you. We've seen it too."

They had also started to sort through everything in her father's apartment, removing piles of garbage that he'd stuffed into every corner and storing boxes of family heirlooms at Nora's house. They gave away or trashed most of his old furniture. Ally offered to move into his apartment at the end of the month, at least temporarily, so they could cover all the expenses of running the place.

Despite their father's absence, the smell of menthol ciga-rettes hung in the air. It would take a long time for it to fade— even longer for the echoes of his heavy-handed demands. At least Lucy wouldn't have to grow up under his strict control. Her daughter would only know the truth from now on, including what she'd seen at Gabriel's house... when the time was right. Her family's connection with the afterlife wouldn't end—not yet —but it would never be the same.

Nora removed her boots and coat. Lucy was on the front rug

playing with Blanco, a deck of Nora's old tarot cards spread out like a fan in front of her, most of them upside down. Blanco was purring beside her while flicking his tail. Neither of them seemed to notice when Nora stepped inside.

Daniel was there with Ally. He'd arrived at the parlor earlier that Saturday morning to help her install a new sign on the front of the building. The lights were bright in the front room, and all the windows were uncovered—a far cry from the intentionally dark interior her father had demanded only weeks before.

"They've been playing for almost an hour," Daniel said, standing up from one of the chairs in the front room. He looked worn out, while she'd taken the opportunity to sleep for another two hours, for once.

"What are they doing?" Nora asked.

"She says she's trying to teach him something," Daniel replied.

Nora's brows went up, and she glanced toward Lucy. "You're teaching him to read tarot cards?"

"He's curious," Lucy said. "He wanted to know how it's done."

"And you know?" Nora asked.

"Grandpa taught me, remember?" Lucy said.

Nora met Daniel's gaze. She could see the irritation on his face as he rubbed the back of his neck.

"I don't think we need any more tarot card readers in our family," Daniel said.

"Then what's he going to do?" Lucy asked as if her suggestion made perfect sense.

"He can be our mascot," Ally answered from across the room.

"Mascots are boring," Lucy said.

"Yeah, but everybody loves a mascot," Ally replied.

Lucy turned suddenly and beamed up at Nora. "He likes you now, Mommy. He said so."

Nora slipped into a pair of comfortable shoes near the door, then went to her daughter and crouched down beside her. "What else did he say?"

"He said he doesn't like sitting around all the time doing nothing."

"Is that so?"

Lucy nodded. "He wants a job, a real one."

"We can't pay him much," Ally said.

"He doesn't need money," Lucy said.

"What should he do?" Nora asked Lucy, watching her daughter's face as Blanco yawned and glanced away from them.

"He wants to protect us," Lucy said. "He wants to be a police officer."

Nora laughed. "Blanco the Cop? That's interesting."

Lucy wasn't amused. "He's serious. He said he wants to protect us."

Nora nodded. "I accept Blanco as our security officer. He's always by the door anyway. He can let us know if anyone bad comes in."

Lucy petted Blanco's fur, running her fingers down his back and then all the way to the tip of his tail. The cat's back arched until Lucy lifted her hand away. "Do you like that, Blanco? You have to protect us now. But you can't fall asleep."

Blanco shifted in his seat, tilting slightly onto his side, revealing the symbol that Gabriel had branded into the side of his chest. Lucy didn't seem to notice it in that moment, but Nora couldn't look away. How had Blanco survived the horrifying ordeal?

Gabriel was a very disturbed man, but he'd lost his wife, and then his daughter. She could *almost* understand how a parent's grief could have twisted him so far. How far would she have gone in a similar situation with Lucy? Wouldn't she have done everything in her power to connect with her one last time?

Gabriel's twisted rage had almost taken Lucy's life, and hers, and now Blanco was part of their family. Another child. An animal that had endured incredible cruelty. And somehow, he had survived.

Somehow, *she* had survived.

THE DARK COVENANT SERIES CONTINUES HERE WITH THE Last Medium: Dark Covenant Series Book 2! Available now!

Read more books by Dean Rasmussen on Amazon.com!

PLUS, get a **FREE** short story at my website!

www.deanrasmussen.com

★★★★★

Please review my book!

If you liked this book and have a moment to spare, I would greatly appreciate a short review on the page where you bought it. Your help in spreading the word is *immensely* appreciated and reviews make a huge difference in helping new readers find my novels.

The Last Séance: Dark Covenant Series Book 1
The Last Medium: Dark Covenant Series Book 2
The Last Demon: Dark Covenant Series Book 3

Shine House: An Emmie Rose Haunted Mystery Book 0
Hanging House: An Emmie Rose Haunted Mystery Book 1
Caine House: An Emmie Rose Haunted Mystery Book 2
Hyde House: An Emmie Rose Haunted Mystery Book 3
Whisper House: An Emmie Rose Haunted Mystery Book 4
Temper House: An Emmie Rose Haunted Mystery Book 5
Raven House: An Emmie Rose Haunted Mystery Book 6
Amber House: An Emmie Rose Haunted Mystery Book 7

Dreadful Dark Tales of Horror Book 1
Dreadful Dark Tales of Horror Book 2
Dreadful Dark Tales of Horror Book 3
Dreadful Dark Tales of Horror Book 4
Dreadful Dark Tales of Horror Book 5
Dreadful Dark Tales of Horror Book 6
Dreadful Dark Tales of Horror Complete Series

Stone Hill: Shadows Rising (Book 1)
Stone Hill: Phantoms Reborn (Book 2)
Stone Hill: Leviathan Wakes (Book 3)

ABOUT THE AUTHOR

Dean Rasmussen grew up in a small Minnesota town and began writing stories at the age of ten, driven by his fascination with the Star Wars hero's journey. He continued writing short stories and attempted a few novels through his early twenties until he stopped to focus on his computer animation ambitions. He studied English at a Minnesota college during that time.

He learned the art of computer animation and went on to work on twenty feature films, a television show, and a AAA video game as a visual effects artist over thirteen years.

Dean currently teaches animation for visual effects in Orlando, Florida. Inspired by his favorite authors, Stephen King, Ray Bradbury, and H. P. Lovecraft, Dean began writing novels and short stories again in 2018 to thrill and delight a new generation of horror fans.

ACKNOWLEDGMENTS

Thank you to my wife and family who supported me, and who continue to do so, through many long hours of writing.

Thank you to my friends and relatives, some of whom have passed away, who inspired me and supported my crazy ideas. Thank you for putting up with me!

Thank you to everyone who worked with me to get this book out on time!

Thank you to all my supporters!

www.ingramcontent.com/pod-product-compliance
Lightning Source LLC
Chambersburg PA
CBHW021130190726
48288CB00008B/2578